EDDIE DE OLIVEIRA

SCHOLASTIC INC.

NEW YORK TORONTO LONDON AUCKLAND SYDNEY
MEXICO CITY NEW DELHI HONG KONG BUENOS AIRES

No part of this publication may be reproduced in whole or
in part, or stored in a retrieval system, or transmitted in any
form, or by any means, electronic, mechanical, photocopy-
ing, recording, or otherwise, without written permission of
the publisher. For information regarding permission, write
to Permissions Department, Scholastic Inc., 557 Broadway,
New York, NY 10012.

ISBN 0-439-54655-9

Copyright © 2004 by Eddie de Oliveira.

All rights reserved. Published by PUSH, an imprint of
Scholastic Inc., 557 Broadway, New York, NY 10012.

SCHOLASTIC and associated logos are trademarks and/or
registered trademarks of Scholastic Inc.

12 11 10 9 8 7 6 5 4 3 2 1   4 5 6 7 8 9/0

Printed in the U.S.A.   40
First Scholastic/PUSH printing, February 2004

For my mother and father

ACKNOWLEDGMENTS

First and foremost, thank you to David for suggesting I write the novel in the first place, and for support throughout. Hearty thanks to Mark Broughton, without whose proofreading and criticism *Lucky* would never have been finished. A big hand for the cast and crew of *Lucky* in 2001. Also thanks and appreciation to: M. Tigana; Lisa Neeley, for advice and encouragement; Ira Potter; Cartwright Jones; Carlo Dusi, for legal tooth-combing; Michael Newton, for authorly advice; my parents and brother for putting up with it all; and the irrepressible Elliott Bravado. The Bravado will be back. . . .

OPENING SKIT

The first time I was fancied by a bloke was during my last year of school.

Josh and I had known each other since we were eleven, which, I was recently told, is around the time Brenda claims she "figured me out." Second to my mother, Brenda is currently the most important woman in my life. She has been my best friend since primary school — always the first to advise and guide, protect and defend. Although I never really opened up to her very much until recently, the point is I've always known I could if I wanted to, despite some moments of appallingly mongish behavior on my part, and I'll always be grateful for that. She knows me better than anyone, and has been a great help in putting together this 400+ piece jigsaw my life seems to have become. And she was the one who, last May, broke the news that Josh had the hots for me.

Joshua Davenport was seventeen when he told his best

friend that he was gay. Apparently, he'd known since he was five that he was different, and since nine that he was attracted solely to boys. He said that he had lived "eight years of hell," unable to be honest with anyone, feeling guilty for his "perversion." He hated life and was desperate to get out of the prison he'd built for himself, so he decided that coming out to his best friend in the strictest of confidence would be a good idea. But this is a comprehensive school, and when you say to someone, "I'm telling you this in the strictest of confidence," what you really mean is, "I'm telling you this in the vain hope you won't open your big gob and tell your friends, who in turn will tell their friends, so by Friday the entire town will know my secret." Inevitably Joshua Davenport was outed within hours and had little time to prepare himself for the vicious teenage onslaught that followed.

He'd chosen the worst time in the academic year to come out. It was just a couple of weeks before the GCSE, AS, and A Level exams began, and tensions were high. Even the thick kids who couldn't give a toss about exam results had been infected by the mood of high anxiety at Lockham High School. So it's no surprise that poor Josh was routinely teased, pushed, spat at, and abused in the days that followed his revelation. He was harassed constantly throughout the two weeks of exams, and the teachers knew this but did little to help. I sometimes wondered if any of our teachers were gay, and even if they weren't, how could they just stand back and watch such appalling bullying going on without lifting a finger? It seemed to me that discriminating against someone's sexuality was the only form of bullying still considered acceptable.

I had always been fairly good friends with Josh. I wouldn't

2

say he was a close mate, and we didn't see each other out of school unless we happened to have been invited to the same parties, but we always had plenty to say to each other, and I felt comfortable around him. Neither of us seemed to be trying hard, which we often did around other schoolmates. But after he came out, I found myself succumbing to the attitudes of the other schoolkids — or, at least, succumbing to my own fears. I began to ignore him in the corridors, watching unhelpfully as other kids taunted him for being a "bum bandit," "faggot king," "back alley boy," or "shirtlifter" (and those were the least offensive insults). I stopped being his friend. And thinking about that now, a little more than a year later, makes me feel all empty in my stomach. I let him down.

The A Level exams started a fortnight after Josh's outing. I sat two English, two History, and two Media Studies exams. In between these nightmares, on the sort of sunny day so pleasant it made you immediately think, *Sir, can we have our lesson outside today?* I was having my packed lunch with Brenda on one of the school benches. Her appearance — that day like all others — was like her personality: no nonsense. She wore very little makeup, looked fashionable in a simple way, and had a short, strawberry-blond cut that really suited her.

As she bit into her sandwich she turned and stared me right in the eye.

"Joshua Davenport fancies you. You lucky bastard!"

I stared back. I couldn't believe I was hearing this. My reputation was surely ruined — I would face the same humiliating destruction that poor Josh had been subjected to.

"Shut up. . . ." was the best I could come up with, as I munched on a Scotch egg.

"He fancies you, Sam. Told me and the girls yesterday. You're well and truly in, you've done so well for yourself."

Looking back, I realize Brenda just assumed I would grab this opportunity and get it on with Josh, but there was no way that was going to happen. I had my public image to protect. And besides, boys were . . . not my thing.

"What do you mean, 'well for myself'?" I asked, not expecting any kind of answer. "I don't fancy him. I don't fancy boys, Brenda — you know that."

She was relentless in her enthusiasm:

"Don't you think it's even a bit exciting? First out-of-the-closet gayboy at school and of all the fellas he chooses you."

I did feel a pang of excitement at the time. There must have been five hundred boys at Lockham High, and with my spots, imperfect nose, and skinny physique it was quite an honor to be fancied by anyone at all, although I'd have preferred it to have been one of the fit girls.

"I don't care. I realize he's good-looking, I just don't feel attracted. I've always been attracted to girls, not lads. In fact, I'm feeling slightly sick at the thought. And no, I don't mean that homophobically or anything. It just . . . makes me uneasy."

Brenda looked stunned.

"He only fancies you, for Christ's sake. It's not like he's gonna roger you!"

She'd done it. She'd mentioned what two men do with each other. I didn't want to hear about that, and was firmly on the defensive now.

"I don't fancy him, OK? What's so wrong with that?" I snapped.

"All right, you don't have to get narked about it. You can be a right mong sometimes, Sam."

As always, the minute Brenda saw that she had upset me, she backed off and resorted to an insult like "mong," which she meant no harm by. That was the last time she mentioned Josh. But behind my back, she told him I had a free house that night (my mum was at one of her triweekly line-dancing classes), and recommended he pay me a visit. She actually told him, I later found out, that "Sam might be up for it if you catch him alone." I think that, as well as playing Cupid, she was conducting her own social experiment into boys' sexuality. I knew nothing about any of this matchmaking until the doorbell rang that night. I was taking a well-earned break from revising the domestic policy of Benjamin Disraeli, flaking out in front of *EastEnders* on the television. I assumed it was my mum, coming back for her cowboy hat or boots. I opened the door, and there he stood. I could smell his Calvin Klein aftershave, and noticed he'd put an above-average amount of gel in his hair. As for me . . . my face most probably looked like I had just swallowed a wasp. I was terrified, which is so ridiculous because a few weeks earlier I had felt so relaxed around him.

"Josh . . . hi! . . . *What are you doing here?*"

"Well, I'm just fine, thanks . . . how are you?" His confidence surprised me, but he was absolutely right — I was being blatantly rude.

"Sorry . . . come in, come in."

I led him through to the living room.

It was all so tense, it was horrible. We killed the small talk (during which I noticed several cuts and bruises on his face, the scar of the bully boys) and just sat watching the telly. Me on the couch, him on the floor. He looked over at me a few times, and I just stared blankly at the screen, as if ignoring him would make him go away. I'd built this barrier in my mind against being who I was, against being me. I suppose he realized all of this, and probably thought I was up for some action if I could get over being scared, like he had been when he lived a lie all those years. So he came up onto the couch and edged closer. I remember smiling embarrassedly as drops of sweat slid slowly and teasingly down my back. I moved further and further down the couch away from him until I fell right off and — BANG! — landed on my arse.

"Shit, are you all right?" he asked me.

"Yeah, bit tired, I suppose."

"Oh, sorry, didn't mean to keep you up or anything." Always so polite, was Josh.

"No, it's not your fault."

"Not yours either," he said.

"What?"

"Nothing."

He was teasing me for being so scared of him. But he was right. If only I could have been more honest with myself back then, but I couldn't. I just couldn't. The fear was paralyzing.

"Um, I've got my last exam next week. History. I'd best get some revision done, I guess."

I was lying through my teeth. I felt awkward, embarrassed, and vulnerable, and blamed Josh for it. He looked as though he had been punched in the face.

"OK, no problem. Thanks for having me . . . over."

I showed him to the door.

"See ya, then . . ."

"Yeah, see ya," he said, and what followed was Josh's last, bold attempt to let me be myself. As I opened the front door, he hesitated, then leaned his head forward just an inch or two from my mouth, locking his eyes on mine. I was aware of what he was trying to do, but wasn't angry, because I realized he knew me better than I knew myself. He could see I was scared, and tried to help me with it. But I couldn't do it. I couldn't let him kiss me. I stepped aside and looked to the floor.

"Well, see ya, then . . . take care," I mumbled.

"Yeah, you too."

Josh left, looking totally crushed, and it was all my fault. Suddenly, and completely uncontrollably, a fit of anger seized me. I screamed out loud and punched myself in the stomach, on the chest and arms. I stamped my feet, punched the couch, slapped the kitchen table, and pulled at my hair, before collapsing onto an armchair and, again unexpectedly, bursting into tears. He was going to kiss me, and that upset me, but I couldn't put my finger on why. I never spoke to Josh again. But I've never forgotten a single bit of that evening. I've thought it over a hundred thousand times in my head. And never told anyone.

Josh had the royal shit kicked out of him at the end of the school dance the following week, which he arrived at by himself. I guess he couldn't really have brought a date. The poor sod was bleeding from three different places on his head, his tuxedo ripped and shredded. His best friend — the same one who told everyone he was gay and put him in the shit in the first place — drove him to casualty. Josh refused to press charges, and although the Headteacher knew which kids were guilty, they had already left school so no action could be taken. I got hideously drunk on white wine and beer, and pulled the first girl I found who was equally pissed. And it worked.

That night, I crashed at Brenda's. She and her boyfriend, Pod, had just had a blazing row and, after drunkenly consoling her, I slept in the spare bed, which was right next to the cot where Brenda's baby brother slept. At about three A.M. my head hit the pillow, and I was in that trippy state somewhere between being hideously drunk and passing out, whilst at the same time seeing everything around me spin at breakneck speed. I could see one thing clearly, though, and it was a sight that just wouldn't go away: Josh.

I saw him in my living room, smiling, then I saw him glancing at me across a classroom, then I saw him at the dance, and finally, most frequently, I saw his face, beaten black and blue.

Brenda's brother shuffled underneath his blanket, accidentally touching the button on a bright plastic toy nestled beside his head. A little tune started. It was the one that goes "If you're happy and you know it, clap your hands." It reminded me of being in nursery school, when all the teachers made us sing along. It made me really sad. It made me want to be that little kid again, when nothing mattered and I didn't have to get all worked up about what I was or wasn't feeling; back then I behaved as I wanted, unaware of what was "good," "bad," "sick," or "wrong." The tune kept playing in that tinny, artificially high-pitched tone that kids' toys make. I looked at the boy and wondered if he would grow up to suffer these terrible confusions, to have the shit royally kicked out of him, and to feel so totally inadequate and worthless.

And the tune continued, its silent lyrics of joy mocking me as my head bore into my pillow, as the room spun and spun.

And the baby slept on, tranquility and peace across his face. If fate had dealt him a future of hatred, fear, and loneliness, he didn't know it yet.

And, feeling scared and lonely, I cried for far longer than I ever had before.

CHAPTER 1

AT MY CONVENIENCE

My name is Sam Smith, and I've never forgiven my parents for it. So short, so simple, so alliterated, so . . . English. Just a hint of foreignness (Sam le Smith?) or a first name that didn't start with an S (I've always quite liked Bernard) would have been a better start. I never got the piss taken out of me for my name — apart from a few of the smart kids at school telling me I was a member of Hitler's SS, which I think was just them showing off they knew who the SS were — but I've always felt it's decidedly average.

It is a warm and musky August day, and I am sitting on the toilet down at my local park. It's 4:28, and I've just played in the single most important game of our season — the annual Summer Cup match against our bitter local rivals, Lockham. My team is the Surbiton Rangers, and I've played for them since I was sixteen — that's three years of twice-weekly training, weekly games from September through May, and the annual

Cup game in August, a match that means more to most of us than the league championship. The park I speak of is here in leafy Surbiton, a smallish town in Surrey, a county that overlaps with Greater London. England is particularly crap about definitions and boundaries. Even our capital city is a mysterious, sprawling mess — London could be anywhere within the M25 motorway, or anywhere within zone 6 of the Underground, or anywhere with a 020 telephone code. Well, I fall into zone 6 and the 020 code, so as far as I'm concerned, although my address reads Surrey, I'm a Londoner. Surrey is a posh, suburban shit-hole; it has no street cred, is seen as a playground for the rich and famous, and is populated by Jeep-driving mums and small-dicked bankers who drive around in large, petrol-guzzling Jaguars. At least, I presume they are small-dicked. I can honestly say I have never seen a banker's penis.

If I've got stuff on my mind, I like to come down to the loo to think things through or, as is the case today, to reflect on a particularly eventful summer. I do like the toilet. At about age twelve, I made a life-altering discovery. The sort of thing that really does change you, your relationships, your friendships, the way you are. I discovered that the best place to think — the only place to think — the place where all your thoughts flow and where you can find quality time to sort things out — is the toilet. I only really feel I can think properly on the shitter. Clear bowel, clear soul, maybe. I feel genuine. When family get-togethers get too much, I head for the WC. When a night out becomes raucous, and the drinking games start, I make a bee-line for the sanctuary of the lavatory. Here I can dwell, contemplate, fraternize, wonder, imagine, and envisage without being disturbed. Apart, that is, from the rare occasions when a drunk bangs furiously on the door, or a toilet cleaner informs me I've spent over twenty minutes inside and asks if I'm misbehaving.

The chaos of confusion began properly at the end of June, just as my first year at university was coming to a close. My mum couldn't afford to send me to a far-off university and pay for my travel to and fro, so without complaint I settled for a place at the respectable local college to study history, a subject I've liked as long as I can remember. I was always very lucky at school, often coming top of the class in English and history, suffering only in maths. I try to read regularly and like to think that maybe one day I can put my degree to good use and become a journalist, or a teacher, or maybe devise a unique online history database covering major events from the year A.D. 0 to the present, with flash-animation re-creations of major battles. My future isn't something I've spent too much time seriously considering.

Some of my school friends went on to further education, some didn't. Brenda moved to Manchester to read philosophy (bloody big waste of time if you ask me — she'd win arguments with Plato, Socrates, and anyone else), and her boyfriend and my old mate, Pod, went up to Leeds to read maths. Mikey White Jeans started working at a mobile phone shop, and within two months he was store manager. He's earning good money, and I see him regularly at football training, although our social lives have drifted a bit of late. Mikey has been known as White Jeans since he took to wearing the aforementioned item of clothing every single weekend for a year when we were sixteen. Mikey thought it made him look fly. Thankfully, the infamous white jeans appear rarely nowadays, but the name is his forever.

So like I say, the end of June. I was sitting in exactly the same place I am now — on the khazi down at the park. I had with me my Chambers Pocket Dictionary, and in it I found a most unhelpful definition for the word *friend*: "one joined to another in intimacy and mutual benevolence apart from sexual or family love." Marvelous. Enlightening. But why apart from sexual love? I mean, what kind of a crappy definition is that? Does that mean lovers can't be friends? That one-night stands don't happen between friends? And anyway, what's more "intimate and mutually benevolent" than a wank between mates? I slammed the dictionary shut.

Nineteen, I thought. Nineteen years old and still sexless, apart from a brief fumble with a holiday girl in Crete two years previously. I was really feeling the pressure to identify my feelings, to understand just what a "friend" was, and whether friends could touch each other without that making them into partners. And just what the hell is mutual benevolence?

To think *they* say it's just a phase. Well, I've been waiting to grow out of this phase since I was eight! I resumed my furious leafing through the dictionary in search of a word that accurately summed up my thoughts at the time. *Bisexual* seemed to be a term of description used only by teenage girls who occasionally snogged each other whilst waiting for big, strong rugby players to shag them. It was also commonly adopted by gothic teens and young people who were totally straight, but just wanted to be different and grab some attention. The kind of teenager whose life was, in fact, perfect and prosperous, so they had to find something to have a problem with. . . .

So bisexual wasn't it. I tried finding *omnisexual* before realizing it implied I wanted to shag everybody, which I don't. Not yet, anyway. *Multisexual* sounded nice and vague. *Unstraight?* That could be good. But none of these words were listed, and once more I slammed the dictionary shut in frustration. If it's not in the dictionary, how can it exist? And yet love is in the dictionary, even though no one knows how to describe it.

The reason for all this consternation was simple. For the first time in my life, I was admitting to myself that I thought I might possibly in effect maybe potentially have the capability to fancy boys. OK, so it was a long-winded admission, but it marked severe progress. I knew, and always had, that I fancied girls. But this summer I began having doubts. Was that attraction just a front? Was I pretending to like girls when in fact I liked boys and only boys? Looking back at my seven years of secondary education, my eyes seemed to linger longer on the boys, not the girls. But was that just because it was a forbidden thing, and breaking rules is so much more fun than keeping to them? Taboo is fun, after all. My keen interest in the changing rooms might have been because I knew far less about boys and sex, and was curious to know more. I knew about girls, had consumed plenty of porn, and enjoyed my holiday fiddle in Crete, but boys remained a mystery.

These confusions were made all the more complicated by being a principal part of the laddish football team. But I decided it was time I figured everything out because I'd spent the previous eleven years trying to get an inkling as to what I was — after all, if you don't know yourself, how can you be yourself? And if you can't be yourself, how can you be what you want to be? I tugged the loo roll angrily and shouted out loud, "What the fuck am I?" But "What am I?" is a bloody difficult question for anybody to answer, let alone a nineteen-year-old leading goal scorer of the local football team with potential for fancying boys. And, where I'm from, blokes are blokes, women are women, and anything in between is most seriously frowned upon. Not so in Greece, where, apparently, men kiss each other when they meet. Here you're labeled from birth: It's black, white, Asian, or other (wow, what an honor to be labeled "other"), male or female, and hetero, homo, or bi. What about that mixed-race hermaphrodite from Puerto Rico, who wasn't black, white, male or female, hetero, homo, *or* bi?

I was pretty sure that I found comfort in breasts. Like many of my peers, I'd always been fascinated by tits, but lately I couldn't help peeking at pecs. And what made all of this so much worse was the fact I couldn't tell anyone a thing. I couldn't express my confusions — or discuss my feelings — with a soul, because of one silly little word, which is so easy to say but so difficult to live with: fear. Being scared stiff. Petrified. What will they say? How will they react? Will they push me away, reject me for good? I had a quiet sob on the lavatory thinking about this. It's so difficult to describe a fear that takes hold of you completely and stops you from doing anything, from being remotely proactive. That's probably the real reason I spend so much time on the loo. I can tell myself my problems, because I feel safe telling myself. Only myself will listen without judging. Or so I thought back in June, anyway. That's the incredible power of this paralyzing type of fear.

Since the first few weeks of the first term at uni last September I'd noticed this bloke who sat opposite me in the lecture hall. He was about six feet tall, slim, with short dark brown hair and stunning brown eyes. His clothes were always smart and casual, erring on the side of trendy, and I knew from seeing him with other students that he was a polite and funny guy. I caught his eye at our second lecture together and just couldn't stop catching it. I really couldn't put my finger on why I kept staring, because he certainly didn't look as though he was as transfixed by me as I was by him. I never imagined him naked or anything. I was just spellbound by him. He seemed . . . what's the word . . . different. It felt a bit like the connection I made with a kid at primary school called Danny Delaney. Without any words, it was clear we had something big in common, and I just knew from the get-go he'd be joined to me in intimacy and mutual benevolence. I knew he'd be my . . . friend.

It took me the whole academic year to pluck up the courage to say hello to him, but hello I eventually said one overcast day on the college campus green. Having just finished our final exam, all the history students had spilled out onto the lawn to lie back and enjoy the sun for an hour or so before heading into the pub for a serious drinking session. The fact that there was no sun didn't dampen our spirits, because the exams were over and it was time to have some fun. We assembled under what had become known as "our tree." It's amazing how quickly you get familiar at uni — we'd been there less than a year and already a great oak was our tree and would always be ours. I noticed "the guy" was sitting by himself just across the lawn. I left my little gang of new friends to join him, gripped by a form of self-confidence I only experience very rarely and very briefly.

"All right, mate?" I said. I always used this as a greeting to blokes. I wanted to say, "Hello, how are you?" but I wasn't sure if he'd turn round and shout, "You a poof or something? You CHATTING ME UP?" and then start spitting at me.

"All right?" was his nondescript reply. He looked at me, expectantly.

"Bitch of an exam, didn't you think?" I actually thought it was OK, but saying that wouldn't have moved the conversation along at all, and by now the realization of the ludicrous confidence of my attempts finally hit me and I began sweating and worrying terribly. I checked my zip was done up. It was.

"Yeah, bit tricky. Mind you, not as bad as the Elizabethan one yesterday."

"God, yeah. That was a real bitch."

I realized I was overdoing it on the word *bitch*. If this guy was like me, if he was also confused, unstraight, multisexual, whatever, I was doing a terrible job of letting him know I was in the same boat. At the moment I was on the same tanker, HMS *Teenager*, struggling through choppy waters, but most definitely not in the same boat.

"I'm Toby," he said.

Toby. I liked it instantly. Two syllables, an "eee" sound that instantly lends a cute factor, and yet still a pretty strong and male name. Nice.

"Sam Smith," I replied.

Why the fuck did I tell him my full name? I could feel a warm redness coming to my cheeks. He smiled at me. I enjoyed him smiling at me, and like a lot of things in my life at that time, I really couldn't decide why. He invited me to sit down, and we embarked upon a round of small talk. He was from Maidstone in Kent, but hoped to stay in his Surbiton student house over the summer, working part-time at the small local factory, where he hoped to be given the thrilling task of packing biscuits. I explained I had always lived in the area, but in a few different places. I told him I went to the local schools and mentioned my local friends.

Then we started talking about our parents.

"My dad walked out on my mum when I was seven," I said, quite bluntly. I don't know where my frankness came from that afternoon. But it had something to do with Toby's calming presence, his aura. None of my uni friends knew about my dad's adultery, and I'd gotten to know them quite well over the year. Yet suddenly, having only just met this bloke, I was telling him all about myself and my family. It's hard to describe why I did it — it just felt so right, so natural. So I carried on.

"He ran off with a younger woman. I've hardly seen him since, maybe once a year. My mum's a star, though. She's done really well on her tod. I'm dead proud of her."

This felt so easy. Toby was the same age as me, and had lived in Maidstone all his life. Coming to university in Surrey, although it was only Surrey, marked a big change for him. He told me his parents were "a bit old-fashioned," which I thought might be code for "they wouldn't approve of my private life." He didn't get on great with his parents — mum a part-time accountant, dad a copper. He proceeded to show me some of his dad's favorite police moves — armlocks, headlocks, and the like. I didn't ask him to, so why he decided to put my head in a painful vicelike hold is beyond me, but it was a novel way of getting to know someone. After assuring me, "It totally immobilizes you," he let go and asked if he'd been too hard. I smirked at the innuendo, and asked if his dad had taught him those tricks.

"Oh yeah, since I was twelve he's been showing me the

ropes. Thinks I'll become a copper too. Not a chance, I tell him. I'm not bitter enough!"

We both laughed at the truism.

"Before my folks got divorced, *my* dad taught me football tricks. I feel like I've missed out now," I joked.

"Nah, football's much better." We both sat back down on the grass and, at last, the sun began shining through those heavy, sagging clouds. "Do you play now?"

"Yeah, I play striker for the local team. The Rangers."

"I keep meaning to play," he said. "But, you know, there are arse issues."

I was totally miffed. Did he mean he kept looking at the other players' arses too? Soul mate! Or was his arse embarrassing in some way?

"Arse issues?" I asked tentatively.

"As in I can't be. Arsed."

"Oh." We both chuckled a bit, out of nerves more than anything else.

Sensing an awkwardness (despite feeling relaxed in his presence, I was still inexplicably nervous too), Toby entered into some small talk again — favorite music stars. He surprised me by confessing to a liking of inane, manufactured pop. I disapproved. Then he posed what seemed like the most loaded question of our conversation:

"What do you think of boybands?"

I avoided eye contact, put my hands in my pockets, and shrugged.

"Not my thing, really." What was he getting at?

He chortled, and continued. "They're all the same. They've

all got a lead singer whose head is stuck up his own arse, then a hard one who gets into trouble, an ugly one who wants to be taken seriously, and always, without exception, there's a gay one."

I smirked but didn't look at Toby. I knew he was shifting the conversation in a new and honest direction, but I was way too scared to take any kind of lead, so I just shut up and let him do all the hard work. Only, he wouldn't let me get away so easily.

"Don't you think?" he asked.

"I suppose. I've never really thought about it."

"There's always a gay one, but there's never a gay pop song," he said, spoken like a true philosopher. He had a point — where *were* the pop songs about being glad to be gay? God knows most straight male pop stars sing enough drivel about their "babies" and looking after their "bitches." Toby continued:

"Hardly any of them come out. They could be heroes, but instead they just do what the music industry tells them to do . . . wear stupid matching suits and sing ballads about girlfriends."

"It can't be easy," I snapped back at my new friend. And we exchanged a look that said everything and nothing at the same time. In a day of inexplicable curiosities, I wasn't entirely sure where my brief anger and surprise came from, but I felt I had to make clear how tricky it would be to juggle fame and private life, and how hard it must be for a boyband celebrity to come out in front of a global audience of millions. But I seemed to be making a statement, saying more about me than about boybands. And Toby sensed that immediately. I felt uncomfortable, vulnerable even, as if I'd given too much away, which was silly because moments earlier I was so at ease. The vulnerability I felt turned into a frosty tension. I seized up. He had been nothing but charming, but I needed to leave.

After a prolonged silence, I terminated our chat with a feeble excuse.

"I'd best be off. . . . My mates and me . . . we're supposed to be going to the pub. Nice to meet you, see you around, yeah?"

"Yeah, sure," said Toby, unconvincingly. As I returned to my friends and the reliable oak, I wondered if I'd upset Toby, if I'd disappointed him, if he was gay or straight, happy or unhappy. I wondered if I would ever see him again, or if by some bizarre twist of fate he'd leave the course never to be seen again. I wondered. And then we went to the pub, drank several pints, shooters, and vodka Cokes, and everything was fine again.

CHAPTER 2

BEER & WORMS

I have always been a big drinker.

I first got drunk at the age of four when I mistook my dad's gin and tonic for a glass of lemonade. Thirsty after playing football in the garden, I downed the glass in one gulp before realizing. Two hours spent dancing like a maniac, much to my parents' bewilderment, preceded an hour of vomiting into the toilet, again leaving my parents nonplussed. Since then it's been a steady descent into the depths of boozing.

Thankfully it now takes a fair amount to get me pissed (maybe around nine pints/double measures) and so I find it a very sociable and relaxing sport to participate in with my friends. I wouldn't say I was reliant on alcohol to have a good time, but it certainly helps. From the age of fifteen, during a marathon cheap-plastic-bottled-cider session down at the park, I formed an unholy alliance with Pod, Mikey, and Brenda. The alliance's main aims were to drink excessively on weekends and avoid getting busted by our parents at all costs. Barring some minor mishaps with tequila, green vomit on white sofas, and being sent home from school while nursing a blinding headache, I succeeded in the aims. We've all always been fond of a drink or two, and it soon became a ritual: school Monday to Friday, drinks at the pub on Friday night, drinks after football on Sunday. During season-time, I avoid drinking heavily on a Saturday night in order to stay on top of my game the following morning, although Mikey insists that a good hangover is as useful as a pair of Predator boots.

So given the alliance's rich heritage of drinking together, I was particularly looking forward to our first session since Christmas. It was the end of June — a few days after term finished — so Toby was still very much on my mind. But I could put him aside in order to catch up with Pod and Brenda, and also Mikey. It was the gang of four reunited.

Of the three, Pod is my oldest — though not closest — mate. He's a phenomenon, the kind of kid who was always talked about at school. Rumors circulated around Pod like overweight girls around poofs. Off the top of my head, I can remember people saying he had shagged a girl six times in one night, eaten a maggot sandwich, wanked in the school toilets every day for a term, and, the one I have tried to forget over the years, sung an excruciating karaoke rendition of Queen's "Bohemian Rhapsody" at his uncle's wedding. The dance floor cleared before the second "Mama" of verse one. Barring the last one, all these rumors were phooey, but the point is people talked about Pod and thought of him as some kind of charismatic living legend of weird. As he's gotten older, he's "normalized" and lost some of that edge. I suppose that's what drew me to Pod when we first met, ten years ago, aged nine — his edge, and the fact he was anything but usual.

Even at nine, my musky summer holidays quickly left me bored and lonely. These two feelings are notorious ingredients for disaster when you're that age. The previous summer, aged only eight, I had decided to rid my garden of ants by creating a complex series of fire traps to fry the creatures. The petrol bombs left enormous black holes in the garden, and even managed to kill a passing blackbird (the first case of a British bird dying in the crossfire, I think). My mum hid all the matches, although I still managed to quench my thirst for pyromania by using a carefully positioned magnifying glass and some old newspaper.

I decided to try to be more constructive with my time that ninth summer.

Having failed once again, one morning I was walking down my road — the same I live down today — clutching my birthday-present football, looking like a typical scruffy nine-year-old boy, when I noticed this shaggy-haired kid sitting on the brick wall in front of his garden, pulling worms apart with long, filthy fingernails. I stopped to watch, and after ignoring me for a few moments, he spoke.

"They grow back together again," he said, with no hint of apology.

I just shrugged at him. He looked up at me for the first time, and I noticed he had these really piercing, powerful eyes on him. Their precise color was difficult to ascertain, although "a kind of hazel-meets-green" provides a decent description.

"I'll leave them on this wall, right? Tomorrow morning we'll come back and they'll be joined up again."

I shrugged again. I remember at that moment feeling really up for getting to know this messy kid better. He was wearing shorts and had a plaster on his thigh. His fair hair was a shambles and his T-shirt riddled with tiny holes, as if a closet caterpillar had gotten peckish and feasted on some Fruit of the Loom.

"D'you play?" I asked him, referring to my football.

He punched the ball out of my hand and began to dribble around me. I became even more fond of him. His movements were hilarious; he looked a bit like a drunken horse trying to juggle. Football definitely wasn't his forté, but he had guts and gusto, and he made me smile.

"What's your name, then?"

"Pod, what's yours?"

"Sam. What's Pod?"

"My name."

"Nickname?"

"Yeah."

I later found out that Pod's real name is Simon. Nobody is really sure quite where Pod came from, but it stuck and, frankly, he'll never be a Simon to me.

The next morning, I walked past his house and saw that the half-worms had disappeared. I knocked on his door and he answered, dressed in a Batman pyjama top and a Superman pyjama bottom.

"Your worms have gone! They grew back and wormed off!" I said, happy for my new pal.

"Told you," he replied, with all the confidence of an expert biologist.

"What's with your pyjamas?" I asked him.

25

He looked down, as if he hadn't noticed the mismatch till then.

"Suppose I get double the superpowers," he said, grinning.

I laughed and laughed.

Pod and I became inseparable that summer, playing every day into the darkness. He enjoyed football, and we'd often involve some of the other local kids in a small game. But he was no superstar striker. In fact, Pod was so bad that I remember his wayward shots smashed many a car headlight. On one occasion, down at the park that would later become home to the Rangers team, Pod managed to misshoot so badly that he whacked a baby full on the back. The child bounced into the air, narrowly missing a nasty bump on the head as it landed. Fortunately for Pod, the sunbathing mother didn't see what happened, and while we were bent over with laughter, she looked around for an explanation as to why her infant was wailing like an angry banshee.

Pod was my bestest friend in those days. My mum and his became good friends, although they're not as close anymore. He joined my primary school the autumn term after I met him, and although Brenda was also a pupil there, none of us were in the same class. I knew Brenda because our parents were friends, but she and Pod didn't really get to know each other till year nine at school, which is around the time I moved further from him and became closer to her. They started going out in year eleven, when they were sixteen. Pod had fancied her for a year, and kept asking me to tell her how he felt. I did just that, but Brenda said she refused to be asked out by proxy. It wasn't until Pod finally plucked up the courage to phone her on Christmas Eve that their relationship officially began.

Despite how different things are now, I still reckon that junior Pod was a really honest and funny guy, and I don't quite understand how things can change so much in a person. We used to be totally relaxed around each other, and say whatever we wanted. Not anymore. I guess it's easier to say what you want when the stuff you're talking about is James Bond, toy guns, and chocolate.

I remember clearly the first time I noticed things were beginning to change around me, and I felt a little different. Later on, I would deal with this sense of difference, of feeling left out, by drinking. But on this particular occasion, I was twelve and hadn't properly discovered alcohol. I had been at Lockham High for just under a year, and Brenda and I were becoming good friends.

Tom, another local kid, was having a sleepover at his house. He invited Pod and me, his two good mates. We liked going to Tom's house late at night because he had satellite TV and you could watch free German porn with these amazing women who were far more interesting to look at than our pubescent female friends.

Tom's parents were always out, and he explained to us that he believed they were part of a "wife-swapping club." Pod never really got this concept, and although I did, I felt more worried for Tom than anything else. I mean, what effect would this have on the poor kid? Maybe it goes some way to explaining his total and full-on obsession with the German porn. Tom was an archivist of soft satellite Euro nudity. He had taped and labeled — in his own secret code — around a hundred porn videos by the age of twelve. But the funny thing was, we used to go around to his place and watch these movies, but it wasn't really a sexual thing. The porno stars were these far-off, glamorous, and beautiful, shapely, developed women who we adored. We gave them all names (Judy, Melinda, Hazel-Pearl) and passed notes to one another in class with messages like "Thinking of Judy's juicies?" Or "Imagine Melinda's tits on your exercise book." But we were twelve, and, for the three of us at least, sex was a far-off country, not accessible by plane, boat, or train. It was a land of pure pleasure and happiness, and we weren't allowed in. But, most importantly, it was a nation we were scared stiff of actually visiting. Projecting our sexual ideas onto Judy, Hazel-Pearl, and the German soft porn made things a lot easier and helped us feel better about our changing bodies and breaking voices.

So Tom invited us over one night while his parents were off at their swingers party. It was just a few days before my thirteenth birthday. Pod and I were slowly, but surely, growing further apart as talk of breasts and condoms replaced worms and favorite chocolate bars. I felt less and less able to relate to him.

Tom raided his parents' drinks cabinet and passed around a bottle of sherry, which we all took tiny, ineffective sips from, pretending to glug heartily. It tasted foul, not dissimilar to the cough medicine they gave us at primary school. (I bet the taste of sherry will now always remind me of being aged twelve and watching soft porn. Or maybe soft porn will always trigger the taste of sherry in my mouth, and I'll be sick, like that rehabilitation technique in A Clockwork Orange.)

We settled down at around midnight to watch the latest

piece of crapply plotted nude entertainment from mainland Europe. We talked enthusiastically of moving to Berlin and finding some of these porn stars, paying them to strip naked. Tom seriously considered stealing his dad's credit card to buy us some plane tickets. Some years later, I heard he did use his father's Goldcard to purchase a hundred crates of lager for a house party. The kid wasn't quite right.

We all hid beneath our blankets as we watched the films. Long periods of silence were punctuated with hysterical *boy's voice turning into man's* giggling as the ugliest bloke in the world managed to pull the divine Judy and get a hand on her juicies. This night, however, I didn't join in with the laughter. I felt really awkward and shy. Obviously it had something to do with this feeling of difference, of not fitting in. But the porn didn't do it for me anymore. Before that night it had been a laugh, a giggle, and, like I said, something distinctly *un*sexual. And maybe it's because it had become sexual that I suddenly didn't like it. It wasn't that I was getting on my high horse and thinking this was a terrible, degrading thing for women to be doing — hell, Tom had heard that Hazel-Pearl was on $500,000 a movie — no, it was just that it seemed wrong some-how, and it made me feel a little sick. Pod and Tom were still well into it, but not me.

Pod and I went over a couple more times after that, and Tom was getting stranger and stranger ideas. He had found a toy handcuff in his parents' wardrobe, which he proceeded to use on Pod, who got very angry and retaliated by pouring sherry over his host. The more Pod enjoyed the porn, the more I felt a gap opening up between us. It just didn't feel right. We were broadcasting on different frequencies, listening to each other but probably not understanding much. I started to turn down Tom's invitations, and he became little more than a person I would nod hello to in the school corridor once a week. I remained closer to Pod, but by the time we were about to turn fourteen, we saw less of each other outside school. I had started playing on local and school football teams, and a lot of my spare time was taken up with training. Pod was whiling away non-school hours with a newfound interest in dance music and DJing, which he tried his best at, despite his horselike movement.

We never drifted properly, not like me and Tom did. Pod was always there, and the drinking alliance he, Brenda, Mikey, and I formed meant we were seeing one another more regularly again by year ten, but still there was a distance between us that I couldn't quite figure out, and I always thought that was a shame. Even Brenda couldn't change Pod. His eccentric ways diminished, and he started dressing like everybody else. That was the Pod I met for reunion drinks at the end of June. . . .

The venue was our local, the Church and Abbey, a large and busy pub popular with Surbiton's young. Converted from a derelict cinema in the 1950s, it has its own jukebox (a luxury in most modern pubs) as well as several fruit machines that it is statistically impossible to make any decent winnings on. The landlord, Freddie, usually allows underage drinkers, providing they are over sixteen and a "good sort." As a result of his liberal policy, we have been drinking there for a few years now, and even befriended some of the old soaks who decorate the barstools of an evening. There's Ray, the World War II veteran who predictably tells us how young people have never had it so easy. His drinking partner is the equally lonely Barry, a long-distance lorry driver who is famously anti-Europe, anti-Africa, and anti-Wales. But these old-timers are in a minority; the pub is usually full of good cheer and good looks.

I arrived at the Church and Abbey by myself and, as is the custom if I'm on my tod, ordered a pint of thick ale, something with a ridiculous and suggestive name. Bishop's Finger is a firm favorite, as are Old Leg Over, Cornish Knocker, and Goblin's Gaze. I pulled up a high stool at a high table. Within a few minutes Mikey joined me, looking a little red-cheeked, having already supped a few cheeky ones at home. Mikey's a short, medium-built lad with a mop of brown hair and a badly shaved face. He is the only one of the gang who earns money, and he's been extremely good to us, buying big rounds and making sure us poor students don't go thirsty. So when I asked him for a beer, he returned with two pints and two shooters.

Just as Mikey indulged in a monologue about the slowing down of the mobile phone industry, I was saved by the arrival of Pod and Brenda, hand in hand, looking quite sweet (probably because I hadn't seen them for ages). Pod wants to be a lad, and he looks the part — drainpipe blue jeans, check shirt, and white trainers are obligatory attire for a night out. He's fairly tall and thin, with shaved fair hair (the shambolic mop long gone) and not ugly, but quite rough looking, as if he's on the prowl for a fight. He used to have bad acne, and his cheeks still show the scars.

Pod and I shook hands firmly, and I gave Brenda a big hug, which felt really good. They say hugs are good for you — they release positive chemicals in the brain or something. Whatever. It was just very nice to see her, strangely comforting and even relieving. It was as if at last, since the weirdness of my feelings for Toby began, I was with someone who might be willing to listen to my thoughts. The warmth of the hug was destroyed, however, when The Housemartins' timeless pub favorite "Happy Hour" came on the jukebox. A fine song, but whenever it plays at the Church and Abbey, Mikey feels the need to grab an empty bottle and stand on the barstool doing his best Housemartins impersonation. His voice is by no means bad. Indeed, I wonder if he does it to show us and anybody who's listening just how talented he really is. But there's a time and a place. Like a team of negotiators dealing with a suicidal jumper, Pod, Brenda, and I managed to convince Mikey to come down off the stool.

And so the drinking began, as did the tales of university debauchery, which included some real gems. Your first year at uni — in Brenda and Pod's case their first time away from home — seems to stimulate a hormone in the brain that encourages reckless, childish, drink-and-drug-fueled anarchy. Pod shared with us the story of Ted, a first-year philosophy student who lived on his corridor. Ted downed approximately ten shots of neat vodka before even making it to the bar each night, drinking these solitary Smirnoffs whilst preparing to go out. As a result, he frequently appeared with shaving cuts, zips undone, and buttons inserted into the wrong holes. Ted was also responsible for several counts of vandalism, including the emptying of his bin into the bath, the dropping of a microwave from a fourth-floor window, and the destruction of three roof tiles.

Brenda's neighbor in her hall, Reza, caused a frenzy when he ventured onto the out-of-bounds balcony one late night after smoking skunk. Reza thought it would be a good idea to drop a brick off the balcony onto the busy street below. The brick, so

Brenda heard, hit the windscreen of a parked car, smashing the glass into smithereens. But what pleased Brenda and the rest of the hall was that the car belonged to a megabitch named Jeanette, so once word had gotten around, Reza became a hall hero, evading the police and hall staff.

My tale of university debauchery was rather long and complex, but it involved the local zoo, excessive amounts of beer, and a nude bet. I was not implicated.

These stories were important. I guess it was all about us showing we had moved on, and also about us expressing our independence and liberty after years of "yes, sir" and "yes, miss," following rigid routine and timetable. Sure, we had lectures and seminars to attend, but we were suddenly faced with the schoolkid dream of not having to go, a freedom that meant our futures were now firmly in our hands. We could do pretty much what we wanted, and although I still lived with my mum, I found myself falling into the student clichés of oversleeping, getting addicted to crappy daytime TV, and missing lectures to recover from hangovers. Once everyone had filled one another in on these tales of university life, and Mikey had attempted to tell us again how the mobile phone industry was slowing, we'd drunk a good few pints, and it was then that the table seemed to regress to what had come before these new lifestyles — back to our school personas.

"Let's play Fuzzy Duck," Pod said, triumphantly.

Fuzzy Duck is a classic drinking game. It's also a pile of shit, but when you're determined to get drunk, it can be a laugh. The upshot is that if you mispronounce "fuzzy duck," you have to down three fingers worth (in terms of height) of your pint. After several beers, the chances of articulation and politeness diminish big time. But tonight wasn't the night for Fuzzy Duck. Brenda quashed the idea by saying, "I thought we'd left all that behind" and giving Pod a threatening stare. I agreed.

Ever the clown, Mikey replied, "Time of the month, Brenda?" He knew this irked her.

"Mikey, if you ever ask me that again, I'll squeeze your balls so tight you'll be able to sing treble again."

This was a sharp reference to Mikey's school career as a choirboy, one which was very successful until his balls dropped. It wasn't that his deep voice no longer lent itself to singing. Oh no. It was more to do with the psychological changes you undergo at age thirteen or fourteen when the balls drop. It just ain't cool to be a choirboy. Choir is the preferred home of choice for batty boys and oddballs. Mikey's burgeoning street cred meant he had to resign. Just as a smirking Pod mentioned Mikey's long-gone days as a cherubic singer —

"Yeah, well, I don't like to talk about it," said White Jeans.

"Why? You were a good singer," Brenda said. "Could be in musicals with your voice. Instead you sell mobile phones and get bevvied every weekend."

"I've told ya, football's my trade," said Mikey. "I'm just waiting to be discovered. Why you so narky anyway? One year at college and you're all pissed off. This is supposed to be a reunion. Give it a rest."

Sensing tension, Pod decided drinking was the best way to ease it.

"Come on, then, neck what ya got."

This call to drinks was normally welcomed. But tonight I felt a bit different. As the others finished their pints off quickly, I coughed and spluttered, spraying the table in a shower of warm beer. This was most unlike me. Admittedly, I hadn't done much downing or played many drinking games since being at college, but still, I shocked myself at my poor skills. Something was definitely wrong. Mikey chastised me with a shout of "woofter" while Pod said I was being a "pansy."

Brenda went to the bar, and Mikey began gawping at the girls as they walked past. In Brenda's absence, he was safe. When she was with us, it was inevitable he'd be clipped round the ear for being "a pig."

What happened next was unusual.

"She's changed, don't ya reckon?"

Mikey didn't hear him, but I did. It was strange — Pod had never really said much to me about his relationship or even about Brenda. We were entering new conversational territory here, but I liked it. Pod seemed strangely vulnerable, peculiarly human. Although I wasn't sure what he'd make of my confusion, he was my friend and had been for years.

"Er, yeah . . . she's a bit more . . . angry?" I offered, more a suggestion than a conclusion.

"Yeah. It's been weird, being away from each other for so long —"

"Bird of prey!" screamed Mikey, destroying the moment. He looked at us and apologized, before returning his sights to the glammed-up babes.

"Must be hard, having a long-distance relationship," I said.

"Too right, mate. Sounds like she's been going out more than me, mind."

"You haven't been going out?"

"No, I have, but not as much as her. I mean, from what she's been saying, she's got a whole new bunch of mates, know what I mean?"

Pod was jealous. Jealous of Brenda's new life, a new life that was totally independent of him, and which he was largely ignorant of. I think he was probably worried she'd been cheating on him. I knew she hadn't, and I doubted she ever would.

"Don't worry about it, Pod," I tried to reassure him. "She's still well into you."

"Yeah, I suppose. Yeah, you're right. Cheers, Sammo."

That all felt quite good. Different, but good. It was just a shame that Pod couldn't repeat that slight tenderness and barrier-dropping sincerity when I needed him to.

Mikey, meanwhile, reported the results of his investigative work.

"Lads, you seen the barmaid? Can't be any more than sixteen. I saw her waiting at the bus stop yesterday. I had to cover my crotch with my briefcase —"

"She looks fifteen," I said, interrupting.

"Even better. Under sixteen's twenty points," said Pod, and I looked at him incredulously.

"Is it?" I asked, dreading the inevitable.

"Oh yeah. Seems you need a reminder, mate —"

And so on to the inevitable.

"Well, the Pod Classification is a highly complex structure, Sam. For a basic pull, anything in the sixteen to eighteen age zone is still fifteen points, although that'll change when we get a bit older. Nineteen to twenty is only ten points 'coz that's our age basically. But from twenty-one to twenty-five it goes back to fifteen points, and anything over twenty-five is twenty points. Forty to forty-five is thirty points, forty-six to fifty is thirty-five points, and anything over fifty . . . well, that's just sick."

Pod had a lot of time on his hands at school.

He constructed these point systems regularly when he was single, but managed to fail spectacularly at them. When we were fifteen or sixteen, we'd often sneak into the pub and the local sleazeball nightclub, Honey Jack's, where lots of similarly aged girls congregated by the bar waiting to be bought a drink. It wasn't hard to pull, and Mikey and I managed to rack up some decent points on the Pod Classification, until I woke up one morning when I was seventeen and realized it was a load of bollocks. Pod and Mikey, however, kept on using it. I suppose it was reassuring to know some things never change, but Pod really should have left his Classification behind along with the drinking games. I felt as though Brenda and I — even Mikey — had moved on. Pod seemed stuck in his school days. I took him up on his use of the term "anything" when describing the points structure:

"What do you mean 'any*thing*'? Any woman?"

"What else?" asked Mikey. "She's definitely a twenty-pointer, that barmaid. A bird of prey!" I wondered how Toby would react to these friends of mine, although I sincerely doubted he'd ever have the chance to meet them. I continued to argue with Mikey:

"She's a little girl."

"She wants it!" shouted Mikey, his volume becoming alarmingly high.

"*Thinks* she wants it," I said, and I meant it. I bet if Mikey had tried to seduce her, she'd probably go along with it before realizing what a terrible mistake it was. There's a rush when you're young to go ahead and shag someone older. It's not a good idea. If you're not careful, you'll wake up the next morning and find that you've lost your virginity to Mikey White Jeans.

"Will you give it a rest, Sam? You're giving me the hump. When's the last time you pulled?" asked Mikey, knowing full well it had been a while.

"It's been three months —"

"Aha!" said Mikey, as if for the first time in his life he'd had a good idea. He hadn't.

"What you need is a lady. Now, who can we find for little Sammy, Pod?"

Just as he said this, Brenda returned, reddened with blind fury, hands rather empty.

"Oi! Where's my drink?" asked Pod.

"Jail bait underage slapper! Unbe-fucking-lievable. She ID'd me. Me! *She* ID'd *me*! Little Miss fucking Muffet." We all laughed at this misfortune as Brenda adopted a thick Essex accent for her next verbal assault. "*Sorry, love, we only take passports for proof of age.*" The impersonation of the barmaid was quite accurate. "I could have slapped her little red cheeks!" Brenda shouted through gritted teeth.

"So could I," said Mikey. Brenda slapped him across the arm.

"Shut up, White Jeans," she said, and I agreed with her.

It was all getting very noisy, and very tedious. It never used to be like that. Had they changed, or had I?

Mikey, ever generous, got the round in.

CHAPTER 3

"IT'S A MIXED-UP, MUMBLED-UP, SHOOK-UP WORLD, EXCEPT FOR LOLA. . . ." — THE KINKS

Before the first training session of the summer, and only a couple of weeks after I'd met Toby for the first time, I sat where I'm sitting now, on the cold toilet in the park, to think back to when I was a kid. It's not often you really analyze what happened to you as a small child, but sometimes it's worth doing, because you can find all sorts of explanations for your grown-up behavior. I think it's good to remember who we were at nine and eleven and fifteen.

The day before this particular toilet session, I'd been round Brenda's house, and she'd bought her baby brother an Action Man toy for his third birthday — with the submachine gun, arctic uniform, and replaceable helmets. And it got me thinking . . .

Ten years ago, my uncle bought me the same toy for my ninth birthday. Back then they were far more primitive, of course. They had the eyes that shifted from left to right via a switch at the back of their heads, a white afro, and a dodgy pair of Y-fronts underneath their combat gear (I always undressed them). But that's just it — I always undressed them. And I used to steal when I was nine. I would nick Barbie dolls from girls in the playground at school. I always gave them back, but only after I'd taken off their miniskirt, crop-top, and jewelry, and dressed Action Man in them. But I never left Barbie naked — I dressed her in his military clothes. I thought they both looked quite fetching. Now psychoanalysts would probably interpret this behavior as a surefire sign that I was a small boy curious about cross-dressing. Not so. I've never been very interested in being a woman. I just liked playing with dolls, and I didn't see why I shouldn't be allowed a Barbie doll just because I was a boy. My games were called to an abrupt halt, however, when my mum caught me one afternoon after school. I had put Action Man and Barbie, this time in their original clothes, in my bed and on my pillow. They looked so sweet together. I felt like Cupid. I didn't have a girlfriend of my own, but I'd brought these two celebrities together, in the privacy of my bedroom, where the prying eyes of the media couldn't interfere. I'd created something beautiful. Then suddenly —

"Sam! What on earth do you think you're doing? Whose doll is that?" yelped my mum frantically, shaking my arms. Anyone would have thought I had done something wrong. To her, anything remotely sexual was not to be discussed, thought about, or done. She wasn't always so prudish. Ever since Dad had walked out on us a year and a half previously, when I was seven, she had been a shadow of her former self; she used to be lively, chatty, and so funny. She made me laugh with her stories, which were all made up, taking me on journeys to planets made of fruit, to shops where you paid for things with fish, to playgrounds where children could play on rides all day and all night and it never got dark. She had the best imagination. Then my dad decided he fancied the eighteen-year-old daughter of Mr. Nedved at number thirty-nine. And that was that. They ran off together for a new life in Antwerp. The very day he left, my mum decided it would be best to tell me all the gory details about marriage (but not sex), as she furiously folded bath towels.

"That's what men do, Sam. They hit forty and go mad. That's what happens. It's a fact. So you can look forward to insanity in thirty years' time."

"Thirty-three, Mum," I offered by way of a correction, and also because it was the only thing I could say with any confidence in this conversation of innocence-shattering, adult proportions. She paused from her furious folding, eyeballed me viciously, then resumed her attack on the unfortunate towels.

"He's a pig. A liar, a pathetic pig. Fancy running off with a girl half your age!"

I most certainly did not. A girl my age was scary enough; a three-and-a-half-year-old would just be plain crazy, as well as unable to speak properly.

"Well, she can have him. I'm fed up with him anyway. Stone-age relic, that's what he is. A chauvinistic, misogynistic bastard!"

She screamed that last line with particular enthusiasm, her eyes lighting up and sparkling as if someone had sprayed a ring of petrol around her eyelashes and dropped a match.

And so we became a single-parent family. I love my mum.

She's been so strong, surviving on her own, working, bringing me up. But it's just so hard to talk to her. And that episode with the Action Man and Barbie summed it up for me. She was mortified; to her, I'd broken down the barriers of right and wrong, of good and bad, of boy and girl. In all three cases, I'd behaved like the latter.

A few months later, I had my first Holy Communion. My mother wasn't a particularly devout Catholic, but she thought it would be a good idea. Looking back, I wonder if she hoped it would rid me of any confusion I might have over what exactly young Christian boys should be doing in their bedrooms. (I've since met plenty of devoted Christian boys whose marriage to God becomes a remarkably open relationship when they enter their bedrooms.)

I was very obedient. I went to all the classes, behaved impeccably at my First Communion, and attended the priest's garden party afterwards. My mother was so proud of me — she still has the picture of her and me in the church on her bedroom wall. She'd invited all my classmates from school to the party, including Brenda and my other good friend from primary school, Danny Delaney. Good old Pod arrived with a frog in one pocket and a snail in the other. But it was all so formal and adultlike, walking around in horribly tight suits and dresses. The grown-ups became more and more sloshed, while all we had to amuse ourselves with was jelly, ice cream, and slices of Battenburg. Before very long, running around the priest's tiny garden got tedious. So Danny suggested we, the kids, play kiss-chase.Within minutes the game degenerated into a sordid farce. Everyone was jumping on everyone else, rugby-tackling them to the ground and covering their giggly faces with wet kisses. I witnessed Pod and Brenda's first kiss, albeit a meaningless one. There was no gender division — in fact, Danny was particularly keen on kissing the boys. And that's when my mum turned around to see twelve children, paired off, rolling around the garden kissing each other. This display of wanton sexuality in a Catholic garden was beyond the pale. We all left immediately, followed by my mortified and apologetic mother. The priest kept telling her, "Not to worry, my dear," and there was something unsettling about his grin as he waved us good-bye from his driveway.

In fact, the most significant part of my weird childhood came with little Danny Delaney, the randy instigator of Catholic kiss-chase. It was our last day at primary school. We were eleven years old. Me, Brenda, and Pod were all about to leave for the same secondary school, where Brenda would end up dating Pod in one of the most mysterious and confusing relationships of modern times, and I would meet Joshua Davenport. So it was our last day and we had P.E. last lesson before lunch. The boys and girls were split up into separate changing rooms for sport and swimming. I've never understood this segregation — if we're as innocent as all the grown-ups make out, what's the problem? As it was the last day of primary school, Danny, who was always a bit taller, a bit more grown-up, and a bit better looking than the rest of us, decided to take me on a mission. Our supervising teacher had nipped out to the loo, so Danny seized the opportunity to sneak a peek at the girls getting changed. We slipped through the labyrinthine corridors from changing room A to the door of B, behind which ten girls were slipping into their P.E. kit. Danny looked through the keyhole.

"Jesus Christ!" he whispered.

"Dirty sod . . . what's *he* doing in there?" I wittily remarked. I don't think Danny understood, because he didn't laugh. Instead, he declared that Jane Simpson had breasts.

That was all I needed to know. We could have left then and I'd have been happy in the knowledge that Jane Simpson had breasts. Jane was really pretty, and she was the most advanced kid in our class, an advancement that had unfortunately manifested itself in the most disgusting smell of stale body odor. I didn't know what it was so one Sunday morning I asked my mum why Jane Simpson stank so much since she'd turned eleven. My mum, equating body odor with puberty, and puberty with sex, was dumbstruck. She put down the knife she was using to chop the carrot, and looked up at me with glazed-over eyes.

"Er . . . well, Sam, when girls reach eleven, they begin to change in lots of ways. And one of those ways is that they begin to smell."

Mum resumed her violent, machetelike attack on the unfortunate carrot. And that was that. Puberty in a nutshell. I went on for two years thinking that growing up meant girls changed in lots of ways and began to stink, before I realized that it wasn't just girls.

So yes — there we were. Danny crouched at the keyhole, me standing behind him, Jane Simpson with breasts.

"God . . . Naomi has really horrible underwear. It's got holes in it," said Danny, with a tone of extreme disappointment. I suspected he actually quite liked Naomi, but now realized that her torn underwear would forever provide an obstacle in his quest to marry her. Danny then offered me a look through the keyhole, which I duly took. It was amazing. I'd never seen anything like it, and it taught me more than the previous year spent in the classroom.

What happened next was far stranger, and far more exciting, than what was happening beyond the wooden door of changing room B. Danny, who was now standing behind me as I crouched down and peered through the keyhole, suddenly developed a bulge in his trousers. Now admittedly I wasn't the brainiest kid, but even I knew there was something a bit odd about this. I also remember thinking it was wrong. To me, it was a warning sign; the bulge only happened when I wasn't behaving correctly. Danny just stared down at it, as I turned to look at him. I remember feeling excited about seeing the girls undressing, but an equally potent feeling filled me as I watched Danny. I had no idea what this feeling was, but I guess some useful words to describe it would be fascination, enthusiasm, and — my number one state of mind over the last nineteen years — confusion. I knew all of this was wrong, but that didn't stop my own little bulge from forming.

And just as that happened, the minute or so of silence was broken by the sweetest of noises. The noise of two pursed lips meeting and greeting. Danny had leaned forward and kissed me. Just like that. And then —

"Daniel Delaney! What the fuck is going on?" screamed Mrs. Verner, our P.E. teacher. She was clearly as embarrassed about swearing as she was about what she had witnessed. Danny, ever the bright kid, played on this.

"What does *fuck* mean, Miss?"

"You know full well what I'm talking about!" she wailed with an alarming swagger, as if she'd been knocked sideways by a freight train coming at full pelt.

"I don't, Miss," replied Danny, and for a split second I believed his brilliant charade. Both bulges quickly disappeared, scared off by the sight of this middle-aged woman with yellow teeth and a fiery temper.

"I mean you know full well you were . . . you were . . . joining lips! And by the girls' changing room. You shan't get away with this. Follow me, both of you!"

I wasn't sure if she meant that kissing by the girls' changing room was the problem — would it have been all right had we done it by the boys'? And why couldn't she say kissing? What was she so scared of?

We both got off with a stern ticking-off from the Headteacher, who was far too embarrassed to tell our parents. (I can imagine the phone call—"Mrs. Smith, I caught your son outside the girls' changing room with an erection and another boy on his lips. . . .")

That was the last day I would see Danny Delaney, since he didn't come to Lockham High. I hear he left school at sixteen and moved to central London. There were one or two rumors that he was working as a barman, and one or two others that he was playing bass in an up-and-coming band. It's funny how people can be so important to you at one point in your life, but then completely insignificant just a few weeks later . . . and maybe a little more significant years later.

These recollections were preying on my mind because little had changed by the start of this summer. I still got those bulges at odd and inopportune moments, although of course I knew why. But I didn't know *why*. At eleven, I was fearless, ignorant about prejudice, just doing what felt right. I doubt you're ever as genuine or pure in intention as you are when you're a child. So while I let Danny kiss me and was confused but not worried, I couldn't let Josh kiss me those six years later. And it's by recollecting the moment with Danny that I realized just how significant that moment with Josh could have been. I could have lost all my fears, all my secrets, the pain of lying, everything could have been deleted with one simple move. But I just couldn't do it.

Be it my fleeting relationship with Catholicism, or my mum's lack of a proper explanation, or the generally accepted notion that boys wear blue and kiss girls, I always thought any kind of a feeling — or a bulge — directed at boys must be wrong, a passing phase, something to avoid. Sounds so stupid. I had read all about Stonewall, gay rights, gay members of the government cabinet, but still it felt wrong. Maybe that's why I visited the toilet after seeing Brenda's brother's Action Man. Away from everybody else, with only myself to concentrate on, no one could interrupt me or my thoughts. And suddenly —

BANG! A thud on the door.

CHAPTER 4

"MASH IT UP, HARRY"
— IAN DURY AND THE BLOCKHEADS

"Sam, get your arse out here!"

It was the dulcet Cockney tones of Harry, coach of the Surbiton Rangers. Harry is a big man: fifteen stone, five foot nine tall, a traditional side-parting in his greasy brown hair, and the obligatory nonleague football manager's camel sheepskin coat, which looks like a relic from the cold war, the sort of thing only worn by a KGB operative or a used car salesman in Essex. Harry has so many chips on his shoulder he could open a successful, if rather unhealthy, fast-food outlet. Although only twenty-eight, he easily passes for fortysomething. As a player, he failed miserably, which he claims was because of forced retirement following a serious injury when he was only twenty-one. We all suspected he was just crap. He has coached the Rangers for two years, his main qualification for the job being that he wanted it when nobody else did. We survived for three months without a manager before Harry turned up one Sunday morning, without any announcement, and began barking orders from the touchline. He assumed the title of "head coach" without anyone asking him to, or giving him permission. Still, nobody has challenged him for the job since, and he has guided us to respectable top-half positions in the league for the past couple of seasons.

However, Mr. Popular he ain't. He shouts a lot, is never wrong, refuses to partake of any training exercises, and frequently delegates the more mundane chores (such as liaising with the borough council for use of the football pitches) to his sidekick, the ultra-skinny and odd Morph. The only other "person" I know called Morph is a tiny clay cartoon character who speaks in squeaks. Sadly, our Morph has terribly low self-esteem, and Harry's oppressive ways don't help. About a year ago, Morph responded to Harry's ad in a local newspaper for an "enthusiastic and committed voluntary assistant." He is twenty-two years old, unemployed, and a hypochondriac — tissues, decongestants, and scarves frequently adorn his face. (Throughout the previous year's heat wave of July and August, Morph insisted on wearing a scarf and woolly hat to every training session.) But he's also strangely likable. I guess I feel sorry for him.

After Harry compelled me out of the loo, it was on to the training pitch, which was thankfully not too sodden — if anything, a tad dry. Next to the toilet, there was a changing room, but we were only allowed access during official games, never for training. As a result, those who turned up in normal clothes had to change into their kit in full view of the public, which caused consternation on more than one occasion, usually from oversensitive dads who didn't want their darling little children witnessing a young man removing his shorts. For God's sake. It

49

wasn't just changing rooms — we were also denied goals during the summer months. The council only put them up from mid-August to May (the duration of the football season). This pissed Harry right off, so he made Morph phone and complain on a weekly basis. As a result of this bureaucratic stupidity, we had to train for the Lockham Cup game using cones for goalposts. The height of the goal was determined by how high our keeper could jump. Great.

This was the first training session of a five-week period prior to the big Cup game on August fifteenth. Although the game was of grave importance, the training wasn't as intense as the season training because we knew it was just a one-off match; there was no continued pressure to play well week in and week out in order to stay in the top half of the local league and avoid relegation. Also, it was summer, which usually meant sun, which in turn meant good moods all round. Good moods for everyone except Harry, of course. (To be fair, he was reported as having a good mood once, sometime back in the early 80s.)

By the pitchside were all the familiar faces, most of whom have nicknames. My teammates call me Glam Sam, Sam-the-Man, Sammo. They don't mean anything, and aren't offensive, so what the hell? More original than American sport nicknames. I hear that the Americans' idea of a nickname is to take the player's name and add a "Big" immediately before. So you get something like "Big" Sam Smith. Over here, we apply our mind a little bit, because nicknames are important — they're your own personal label, your teammates' best expression of fondness. In our team we have "Chopper Chubby" Johnson, real name Graham, also known as Fatso, Fat Bob, and Bob. I've never been told why he was occasionally called Bob, but we have a little chant for him on the rare occasions he drifts forward from center back and scores:

He's big, he's round, he bounces on the ground,
Chopper Chub, Chopper Chub.

One of my good footballing mates is Laid Back Steve King, a twenty-year-old guy whose school report once read, "If Steve were any more laid back, he'd fall over." Laid Back, as he is commonly known, is seriously chilled, and famous for his half-time cigarettes, which he claims "help my joint movement." It's always good to see Steve in the left-back spot; he brings his usual mixture of apathy and enthusiasm to the team, and we appreciate it, although he is often the butt of Harry put-downs for being a lazy arse. One minute he pulls off a tackle or clearance of breathtaking beauty, the next he's chatting to the opposition striker and forgetting there's a game going on. Steve King is one of about ten people in the whole of South-East England who is vaguely capable of using his left foot in a defensive position, so he is the only guaranteed starter in any of our games, as there is no competition for his place. Harry resents this.

Also worth a mention is Trevor, the only member of the team above the age of twenty-five. Quite why a forty-year-old with a wife and baby wants to spend two sessions a week and one match afternoon with a bunch of teenagers and twentysomethings is a mystery, but he's an interesting guy. Trevor is an English teacher at a private school nearby, but after a major dispute with the coach of the staff team, he joined us earlier in the year and has remained a stalwart in central midfield ever since. Off the pitch he's witty, kind, and generous, offering lifts home to everyone after training. But this is his Dr. Jekyll side. On the pitch, Trevor undergoes a strange transformation and becomes something of a Mr. Hyde — a crazed, possessed, wild creature, ruthlessly in command of his game at the expense of anyone on the opposing side. Trevor loses his temper at the smallest thing, regularly comes in late for tackles, receives countless bookings, and occasionally dives to win free kicks and penalties (with a 100% success rate, as it happens). It's bizarre. Chopper Chubby jokes that football is like therapy to Trevor — a way of letting out all the stresses put on him by his wife. He's probably right. Trevor certainly lets it all out.

And finally, standing tall, proud, and handsome on the touchline as he warmed up his thigh muscles, was Pretty Boy Pete — the team pinup. Pete is a funny one, because I only ever see him at football. Although he lives nearby, he never seems to be in any of the local pubs, shops, or restaurants — he's something of a hermit, despite his film-star good looks. I've played alongside him since I was fifteen.

Together, and aided by a few loyal others, we make up the Surbiton Rangers, and our favorite motivational chant goes like this:

We hate Lockham, we hate Lockham,
We are the Lockham haters.

Lockham, the local rivals, are, always have been, and always will be s-c-u-m. It's just the way it is. Statistically, they're the more successful of the two sides, and play a league above us during the season proper, although Pod once worked out that our team had bedded more women than theirs, so we were superior. Mikey deduced that we were younger, better looking, and better paid in our jobs than Lockham, which was probably true. But they still won more games. This summer, we were determined to put that right.

Morph laid out some cones ready for us to run around, as Harry barked at us to warm up. He famously demands elaborate warm-up exercises, but never demonstrates them. Given his physique and temperament, that's probably for the best. But it's difficult to understand just what the hell he means half the time. More often than not he berates us for getting his idea of a "sit-up, press-up, star-jump combo" wrong, when a small demonstration would help. He always carries round his leather-bound copy of the *Football Association (FA) Guide to Successful Coaching*, which he used as part of his Coaching Qualification course. Harry is clued up on the theory, but isn't quite as confident with the practical, so sometimes his wild ideas of playing a 2-1-3-3-1 formation don't quite take off. We did our usual sprints, jogs, and warm-up techniques to start off with, as well as some heading exercises. There was a lot of chatter as we caught up on all that had happened in our lives since the season finished in May. It felt good to be back.

All the outfield team take part in shooting practice, and this is always a potential exercise in humiliation. Having not kicked a ball for a couple of months, we were all a tad rusty, but Trevor's leg seemed to have corroded. I struck a few powerful shots straight at our keeper, a tall, mixed-race kid called Nathan (who at seventeen had a bright footballing future ahead of him), and Pretty Boy had some good efforts tipped over the imaginary bar, before Trevor stepped up for his first.

My God.

The ball moved so slowly from Trevor's foot to the goal area that Nathan had enough time to sip from his water bottle before reaching down to collect. Trevor's temper began to slowly boil. He got angrier with himself than with anyone else on the pitch. His second shot was so wide of goal, it hit a couple who were having a picnic some thirty meters away from the football pitch. Their thermos flask full of soup was knocked over, spilling minestrone onto the tartan blanket, and Trevor had some apologizing to do, his red, sweaty face becoming a picture of rage. Laid Back Steve King found this all very amusing — being so chilled himself, he loved it when someone else got stressed.

Trevor's final effort on goal seemed like it was staged for Laid Back's benefit. The ball made a loud and high-pitched pinging noise as he struck it, and it bobbled pathetically along the grass till it eventually reached its destination, somewhere on the road outside the park. Trevor cursed himself and ran to get the ball, while Laid Back lit up a ciggy and laughed like a kid.

Every footballer's favorite bit of training, once you've got the games of "football without a football" and "football tennis" with an imaginary net out the way, is a mini match. This normally takes place about an hour into the two-hour session. Which is about the time, on this particular occasion, that Mikey showed up, wearing the team shirt and a pair of white jeans. Mikey loves football, he eats it and sleeps it, and every other Saturday he's down at Stamford Bridge watching his beloved Chelsea FC play. But he can't stand Harry and Morph, and never has done. He's also never been a good one for authority. As he lumbered to the touchline, the management duo, watching us on the pitch, was not impressed.

"Morning," he muttered in Harry and Morph's direction.

"Afternoon by my watch," said Morph, ever the pedant.

"Sorry, got a bit pissy-boots last night," was Mikey's excuse.

When we were bored in GCSE Maths, me and Mikey would list as many different words and expressions for being drunk as we knew. Pissy-boots was a particular favorite — it sounded like a very 1930s England thing to say. Other favorites included mullered, paralytic, horsed, hammered, rat-arsed, pickled, sozzled, batted, trolleyed, and "alive but in pieces" (ABIP).

"Oh, dear . . . a bit pissy-boots, Morph," said Harry disapprovingly.

"No commitment!" was Morph's clipped assessment.

"Won't happen again," Mikey promised eighth-heartedly.

"Well, the others have managed it. We've got a trophy to win, Michael, and with this attitude we don't stand a chance. I want you here ten A.M. Sunday morning, bright-eyed and bushy-tailed. Got it?" Harry was defiant in maintaining a sense of discipline. After all, when he took over the club he introduced fines for anyone who arrived late three times.

"Sorry, boss."

"Don't mention it."

Morph, who felt as though he should help in these sorts of disputes, contributed something along the lines of "Shoo, shoo!" and with that Mikey was off. Harry could now turn his attention firmly onto me.

"Silly, silly, silly!" he shouted, this being his catchphrase. "Sam, get your arse over here!"

The others played on as I came to the touchline, out of breath.

"What was wrong with that?" I asked, genuinely confused as to what had made me behave sillily this time.

"No, what did I say?" replied Harry, adding to the confusion. I sensed Morph felt he should say something useless and of no substance, and right on cue —

"What did he say? Answer!"

"All right! He said to feet," which was what Harry had told us to concentrate on before we began the training match.

"I said to feet. Now you do know what that means, Sam?"

"Course I do, Harry," I said, my intelligence having been insulted by, of all people, Harry.

"I repeat: You do know what that means?"

When Harry says, "I repeat," it means he doesn't believe you, or he is pissed off at you, or both. In either case, your answer isn't what he wants to hear. So I elaborated for him.

"Ball to feet. Avoid the stodgy long ball game so common in English football of present and yesteryear."

Touché. Long sentences and expressions like "yesteryear" stumped Harry. He wasn't stupid, he just didn't like long sentences.

"What do you mean?"

"Clarify!" squealed Morph.

"You don't want balls in the air," was my layman's description of the ball to feet rule.

"Right. Ball to feet is what I want. Not so difficult — even for you, Sam. Even for a gentle boy like your good self."

This was Harry being cheeky, and this was Harry pissing me off. For the closing months of the last season, when I had already been at college for a while, he'd started calling me "gentle" — his way of describing boys who aren't rugged, physically strong, or particularly masculine. I'm not rugged, I'm not very strong, and, in the words of The Kinks, "I'm not the world's most masculine man." But to call me gentle was provocative and rude. I told him I wasn't, to which he replied with a rant, as he paced up and down the touchline, barely glancing at the game:

"Not gentle! Forgive my rudeness, Sam, but you're hardly Chopper Chubby Johnson, are you? He gets stuck in, tackles hard, gives his all. You may have skill but you lack the most essential thing. Do you know what that is?"

I hate it when Harry asks silly questions, the answer to which could be any one of a million different things.

"Speed?"

"No, bigger than that," said the boss.

"Strength?" A surefire winner.

"Bigger still."

"Commitment?" Harry and Morph always banged on about the team lacking commitment, especially when he saw players walking into pubs the night before a big game.

"No, you've got all of those things. Bigger even than commitment, Sam."

I thought and thought. "Flair?" was the best I could come up with.

"Teeth!" he shouted, spit flying into my eyes. Morph stayed perfectly still beside him. "You don't have teeth, pal. Strong, sharp, vampire teeth. Teeth that show no mercy, that'll bury themselves into flesh and not let go. That'll suck the blood and juices out and mmmm . . . chew up the opposition. Men's teeth!"

This was passionate Harry. Whenever he felt strongly about

something, he became surprisingly, and a little strangely, eloquent and poetic. Morph tended to destroy these verbose moments with inane babble:

"You got no bite!"

"Right, no bite," agreed Harry. "But you will have, you're getting there. Soon as you pay more attention to your feet and not your hair you'll be laughing."

There he went, having a go at my "gentleness." Well, my hair is important to me. No point having any if it doesn't look good. While I whinged inwardly, Harry blew on his whistle. "Quick runs, go!"

Quick runs is what Harry gets us to do when he pulls us out of training. He claims it is because, standing around chatting, our muscles warm down, leaving us in danger of doing ourselves damage when we return to the pitch. So I had to run up to a cone, then back the ten meters or so distance to another, three times. On my third return, he blew his whistle again and instructed me to tackle Morph. I couldn't resist the opportunity to wreak some well-deserved revenge on the beanpole, and at the same time, show some "teeth." I launched an illegal two-footed tackle on the unsuspecting Morph, sending him flying back onto the ground. Morph, who once convinced himself that flies had nested in his skin when he had a mild rash reaction to a detergent, clutched his arm and yelped. Harry wasn't interested in the little guy's theatrics.

"Silence, Morph," he said, giving me a hand up and leaving his assistant to lie in apparent agony on the grass. "Nice one, Sam. Your teeth are growing. Now let's give 'em a good brush up, and sharpen 'em!"

He obviously didn't like what I was becoming — the sweet

and sensitive boy I am today. He preferred what I hated — a laddish loser. I realized after this first training session that my confusions weren't going to be made any easier by Harry and Morph having a go at me. And now that I'd come to terms with a few of my feelings, even if I still found them beguiling, would the ultra-straight team find me out? Would they feel unhappy undressing around me? Would the piss-taking get too much? Should I stand up for myself, or keep quiet?

That was all this summer was becoming. One big bloody question.

CHAPTER 5

GENTLENESS

Three weeks after our first meeting, Toby phoned, and I hadn't the faintest idea who he was.

I was sitting in my living room in a T-shirt and boxers half watching an old movie called *Tea and Sympathy* on the TV when the phone rang.

"Hello," I said.

"Hello. It's me."

"It's you. . . ."

"Yeah, how are you?"

"I'm good, who are you?"

"It's Toby."

"Toby, shit, I mean, fuck, I mean — how are you?"

Once again I had managed to make a complete fool of myself. I had given Toby my number a week or so previously, when I'd bumped into him in the library as we both returned overdue books. He had a job interview so couldn't chat, but we did swap numbers on scraps of paper, and I'd intended to phone him just as soon as I'd spoken to Brenda, sorted out in my mind what he meant to me, and had chosen a suitable pub to meet at — not somewhere like the Church and Abbey where I'd be recognized. I was nowhere near achieving any of these goals, but the call wasn't unwelcome.

"I got the job at the biscuit factory," he said. "Pay's shit, but it's a job. Keep my rent paid for the summer."

After I told him about the weird night that was the reunion session at the pub, we arranged to meet by Our Tree ("our" still meaning me and my university buddies). It was all so impulsive and immediate. Toby phoned at around two, and by three o'clock we were chatting by the tree again, on another marvelous, bright summer's day. He seemed a bit more cheery this time; he was definitely smiling more. I think I was a little less nervous, and I made sure I wore my favorite red T-shirt and gorgeous aftershave in order to give the right impression.

"Fancy a walk?" he asked. I said yes, and we went for a stroll around the near-deserted campus of perfectly kept lawns, cracking wood benches, and new, skinny trees. Apart from a handful of students scattered about, most of them back for exam retakes, it was extremely quiet and ghostly. I quite enjoyed it — it felt like me and Toby were very much on our own, with lots of space to talk and think. I told him about the football training, and how Harry called me "gentle," which he seemed to find quite amusing.

This meeting was different from our first. There was a real sense of calm and relaxation, like we'd worked each other out. As we strolled, hands in our pockets, there was a gap in the banter, which Toby filled with an obviously pre-prepared statement.

"Hey, about the boyband thing . . ."

We both stopped and faced each other now.

"Sorry, was I a bit arsey? Not sure what came over me," I said.

"No, you were cool. I had a think after you left, actually. You were right. It can't be easy, especially if you're famous."

I sensed where this was going, but I didn't feel defensive this time. In fact, I wanted him to keep going, to ask questions, to let me reveal myself. It felt good. But I couldn't say anything for myself, as my next few words proved.

"Lucky we'll never have to deal with problems like that, I guess."

That four-letter word again. Fear. Without really wanting to, I had told a lie. I saw him smirk, and there was another pregnant pause as we resumed our walk, the breeze swimming through us. Then Toby found his courage, and we stopped still again.

"You ever snogged a bloke?"

"Excuse me?"

"Well?"

"No, no, never. No."

"OK."

I felt that tingle all over that you get when you're momentarily embarrassed, like a quick electric shock emanating from the stomach. But I didn't feel paralyzed anymore. I felt as though I could speak.

"Have you?" I asked, pretending not to care too much about his answer.

"Er . . . yeah. Yeah I have. Affirmative," he said, and laughed a little nervously. He started strolling again, and I followed.

I looked at my feet, as if they were the most important thing in the world to stare at. I felt a bit nervous now, as if I was in the presence of a really cool bloke whose leather jacket was better than my hooded parka. He'd experienced life and adventure — he'd experienced snogging a bloke! — while I just sat in pubs and Honey Jack's getting off with slappers whose skirts could easily be mistaken for belts.

"I enjoyed it," he continued. "To tell the truth, I've done it a couple of times."

"Oh," I said, genuinely a bit taken aback, but not upset. "Is it much different?"

"Stubble can be an arse. Hang on, I'll rephrase that . . . stubble hurts a bit."

I laughed excessively, glad of some light relief to this heavy shit.

"You think about it, then?" he asked. The onus was on me now. He'd asked a blunt, direct, and good question. Suddenly, the four-letter word crept back into my body and seized me up.

"No, not really," I lied. "Just curious."

We carried on walking for a couple of seconds. Then I stopped. It hit me. If I couldn't be honest now, with a friend who had himself admitted to snogging a boy, then would I ever be honest? In the space of a couple of seconds, I had visions of me as a forty-year-old married man cruising parks in the hope of anonymous, quick, and dangerous sex with random men. I had horrific thoughts of never living an honest day in my life. So I just thought, *Fuck it*, breathed in, and spoke. At long last.

"Well, I've mulled it over. But then . . . then I think about having a wife and kids one day. And I get all lost."

There. Not so hard after all. And it felt like a massive boulder had been taken off my shoulder. Toby's answer was spoken so softly, so reassuringly:

"You're not the only one. Confused, I mean. What I'm trying to say, and I know it's really difficult, but . . . well, me too. I'm confused. A lot. I don't know what to call myself. Gave up trying ages ago."

I looked him in the eyes.

"So you're gentle?" I asked.

"Yeah, I'm gentle."

I was ecstatic. We truly made a connection; all my suspicions about him had been proven right. What's more, he was the first person who had pried so much personal information out of me, and I'm really not sure how he did it. But I felt like a new boy, a different Sam. He made me feel special.

"Oh, marvelous!" I said. "Let's be gentle together!"

I realized the sticky implications of this statement immediately.

"Not like that! Christ, I don't wanna roger you up the arse or anything. It's just . . . I've met another gentle bloke."

I was genuinely a bit surprised, but more relieved. Apart from Danny and Josh, I don't think I'd ever knowingly met anyone remotely unstraight. I didn't live far from central London, and I knew there was some sort of "scene" there where men held hands with each other and dressed up as women on the streets, but I was hardly going to go and join in, especially not on my own. Some of the lads at school used to talk about the "fag zone" club, a popular nightspot called Bliss, but again it never crossed my mind to go there. I'd heard horror stories about old men feeling up your bum as you walked in. Nasty business. But here, at last, after nineteen years of nothing much exciting happening in my suburban nightmare, along came someone who lived minutes away, who truly understood and, it seemed, cared. Someone who was going through the same anxiety and worry. Someone who probably experienced the same sort of weird growing up I had. Someone who may even have known his own Danny Delaney. I felt calmer and happier than I had in a long time. I carried on excitedly, with animated hands.

"Brenda, she's my friend since primary school, she knows about me. . . . Well, she knew before I did, and my mum kinda hints at it, but no one else has a clue. I'm quite good on the football team, you see, and it'd be a bit of a scandal. If they knew I wasn't one of the lads, they'd probably kill me . . . especially Pretty Boy Pete."

I breathed in. Wow. Not only had I mentioned, for the first time, my real fear of being found out by the lads of the team, but I was confessing my feelings for a teammate! He asked about Pretty Boy.

"Oh, he's well nice. Plays left midfield. He's got short black hair brushed forward, and these bright, blue eyes. Slim but strong and totally straight. I can just tell looking at him. I used to get into play fights with him just so I could . . . you know . . . get close."

Everything about Toby's calm expression, opposite my frantic moving about and hand gestures, seemed understanding.

"You can't look at boys for too long in the footy team or people get suspicious," I said, sensing this was a world he hadn't experienced that much. "I can't help it. Whenever Pretty Boy's got the ball and anyone shouts, 'Man on,' I keep thinking it's an invitation."

This made us both laugh, but I meant it. I once spent an entire training session in smutty innuendo mode, and "man on," which is supposed to alert you to an opposing team member's presence, seemed an obvious call for homoerotic acts. Similarly, "make a pass" sounded like an encouragement, and Harry's request that we "go in hard" was just dirty and graphic. After I giggled at the thought of all this, I went very serious and kneeled on the grass. Toby sat beside me, his legs folded.

"What's wrong?" he asked.

"I've never really talked about this stuff before. I guess it's easier with people you don't know so well." I pulled some blades out of the soil and fiddled.

"You can relax, Sam. Be yourself."

I was in full flow now. "Do your parents know?" I asked.

"Not a clue. I've had quite a few girlfriends, you see, and it keeps them from suspecting. They could never find out about the boys."

I asked him about his use of the plural.

"Well, just one proper boy actually," he replied. "Paul. Stunning he was."

It turns out they met at school, in physics. Of all the classes to meet someone at . . .

"It was a year eleven thing. Couple of months, that's all. And it was brilliant."

He seemed a bit sad. I asked if they "you know . . ." and Toby got my gist.

"Nothing much. We weren't really into that full-on stuff. You know. . . ."

"Oh, me neither," I said quickly, not really knowing what I was talking about. "Can't say I'm into the hardcore myself. You see, that's just it . . . how can you be called a poof if you don't take it that way?"

"Sex comes in different shapes and sizes, Sam." A bit patronizing, but he was right. I guess buggery isn't the be-all and end-all.

Toby explained that Paul was after someone more honest. Toby didn't feel confident enough to go out with him in public. "Except to Old Compton Street," he added, but my baffled expression made him realize he needed to be more specific. "The gay village." I was still nonplussed. "In Soho, the center of London!" he said. "Jesus, I thought you were a bit more advanced. . . ."

I felt really small now. Crushed, even. I really had lived a sheltered existence. I apologized, and he made me feel better by telling me I didn't have to. He asked if I'd experimented, and I told him someone was interested in me in my final year at school, but that nothing much happened, which was a sort of half-truth.

He explained to me that his dad pretended to be a liberal, but that in fact he was quite old-fashioned.

"My parents aren't ever gonna find out about me," he said, decisively. "A promise I made to myself when I was thirteen."

I was surprised again — this time, at the lack of boldness. Toby's bravery helped me be honest with him, yet suddenly he was talking about keeping secrets and living lies.

"But if you're not honest with them aren't you just protecting them? Denying what you are for other people's sakes? Aren't you just satisfying their prejudice?" I asked him with bite.

He seemed a little taken aback, saying something about it being a price he'd be willing to pay. I explained to him how I'd never acted on my feelings before, I'd just felt them. He said that was the definition of denial, and I totally understood. But it was also a lot more. It was being unable to be myself — even if I wanted to be — because I'd been conditioned by those around me, and even by things like TV shows and pop songs, to think straight all the time. Maybe if I'd gone to Old Compton Street when I was sixteen, like Toby had, I wouldn't have been so useless, and so inexperienced too.

But I *was* experienced at football. So I steered the conversation back to to my favorite sport, and it turned out Toby used to play at school, a couple of years back. Knowing that only eleven of us were available for the imminent Summer Cup game, and that Harry always liked to have at least one sub, I invited Toby down to our next training session.

"I'm not fit," he said.

"I wouldn't say that," came my reply. Audacious stuff, but it just goes to show how much Toby had calmed me down. He, however, kept making excuses.

"It's been ages since I've been anywhere near a football pitch."

"You scared?" I asked, playing a bit of psychological ball game.

"Piss off!" He was on the defensive. The tables had turned!

"You are, aren't you? Scared the big boys might beat you? Or scared of your reputation with the little fairy boys who think football's all beer and fights?"

"You really should stop putting yourself down like that. I don't think you're a little fairy boy, you shouldn't call yourself that." Damn. He was good. Tables returned to original position.

"That's how you see it," he continued. "Straight footballers are big boys, poofy Diana Ross fans are little boys. Look at you — you're a poofy little big footballer. Stop labeling."

"You just labeled me!"

"That was different. I was being ironic. I used contradictory labels to sum up the paradoxical stupidity of your situation." He had the gift of the gab, and oozed a self-confidence I could only dream of.

"Stop being so bloody clever," I warned him.

"OK, I'll be a big boy, Sam. Show you what I'm made of. I'll be there."

I couldn't believe it.

"Really?"

"Really. But don't blame me if I'm shite."

CHAPTER 6

ONE SAMMY SMITH, THERE'S ONLY ONE SAMMY SMITH. . . .

I had tried to tell him everything. Tried so very hard but, ultimately, failed. There was one vault at the back of my head that I had attempted to carefully open, but couldn't. Inside the vault there sat this little secret. It wasn't purely an issue of courage; there was also a sense of excitement in the secrecy, a feeling of ownership. I felt open enough to tell Toby about so much, but not this. Subconsciously, I had probably decided that this would be the only thing that would remain truly private. Whenever I thought about it, or it suddenly popped up in my day-to-day, I felt this electric tingle inside. I liked that. And as much as I was getting to like Toby, I just couldn't tell him. It wasn't that I didn't think he would understand — I was certain he would — but I think I wanted to maintain a portion of privacy in the hectic typhoon I found myself standing in the middle of.

I caught Toby's eyes very early on in the first term of our degree course. It would take me until June to finally speak to

70

him. But about a month after I first set eyes on Toby, in October of last year, there was somebody else. In fact, he's still around, in a sense.

For the past three years I have been a season-ticket holder at Litton Park FC, a moderately successful South London club in the English First Division that I have supported since I was a wee nipper. I went with my dad for a couple of years before the divorce, then didn't start going again till I was old enough to go by myself, about six years ago. Back then, Litton Park were a Premier League team, facing the likes of Manchester United and Liverpool week in, week out. That was then. Now they seem doomed to mid-table First Division mediocrity, for as far as I can tell, my team ain't going nowhere.

It's hard sometimes for people to understand the fanaticism football inspires in its followers. But to me it's a part of my life I just can't see myself without. Spectating is more frustrating than playing, because while you can at least try to affect change when you're on the pitch, you can only scream your support (or disapproval) at the overpaid players when you're in the stands. I suppose that's important, though; a lot of professionals claim that the fans' support can sway the result. The way I've begun to think about supporting Litton Park, or any club for that matter, is in religious terms. The stadium is the church, the team coach a god, and his players the disciples, or clergymen. Instead of hymns we have chants, instead of communion we have half-time beer and burger baps. For most loyal fans, football is the only religion, the one true passion in life. Whether that's tragic or not is another matter entirely, but that it is a religious experience is without doubt.

Now whilst our manager is competent and comes across as

71

an affable guy, he is not our god. The man we fans worship is our toffee-skinned, six foot five, glamorous number nine. The Uruguayan center forward, Alvaro Cruz, is the star player who we all adore. Poor Alvaro, who has been with us for a little over a year, often looks like he wants to be somewhere else, but he does the business for us — and always with a smile on his face, and that's important. Possessing the deft touch of a South American, he dances with the ball and pulls off occasional moves of breathtaking brilliance.

Only about a week ago, I had a dream where Litton Park were top of the First Division, and with two games to go, we had clinched the championship, meaning Premiership football the following season. The players were being presented with the trophy and their medals at the end of a 7–1 thriller, in which we destroyed West Bromwich Albion. Alvaro Cruz had scored four goals, and the crowd of around twenty thousand was ironically chanting, "Alvaro for England." He was our hero, and his loyal followers were showing him just how much we cared. So he received his championship medal from some executive and then, for no apparent reason, he began walking over to my section of the stands. The crowd was still clapping and roaring his name out with enthusiasm. I suddenly realized he was looking at me, pointing me out. He waved his hands at the crowd to demand quiet, and they obliged. He stood by the advertising boards, just inches away from me, pointing and chanting, all by himself, to the tune of "Guantanamera," "One Sammy Smith; there's only one Sammy Smith, one Sammy Smith." He gestured to the crowd around me to join in, which they duly did. The chant spread quickly and soon the whole stadium was joining in. In my dreamworld, I suddenly understood the buzz of being adored by tens of thousands of men, women, and children. Alvaro jumped into the stands, came up to my seat, shook my hand, and, in a thick Latin American accent, said to me:

"You are the hero of Litton Park, Samuel."

I thanked him and continued shaking his hand manically. The chant grew louder and louder until it was interrupted by a bizarre high-pitched whine. This annoying noise wouldn't go away, and I had no idea where it was coming from. Then I woke up and turned my alarm clock off.

Litton Park is one of the cheaper London clubs, unlike some West London teams for which you'll need a bank loan in order to offer your support. Litton have won very little in their hundred or so years of existence, a couple of Mickey Mouse trophies and several promotions from the lower leagues notwithstanding. They have always played in the same modest but quaint stadium, which can now fit around twenty thousand supporters. This is peanuts compared to the big English clubs, but the atmosphere is intimate and intimidating for opposing teams. The front few rows of fans are very close to the pitch, and this helps create an electric vibe about the place. I go every other Saturday (assuming matches have not been rescheduled for TV coverage), sit in the same spot, beside the same faces, and enjoy the same displays of occasional magnificence and frequent crapness. Last season something totally weird and out of the ordinary happened.

It was the sixth home game of the season, played on a sharply warm October afternoon. The score was 2–0 to Litton Park at halftime and good moods were out in abundance. The sun shone, the hot dogs and ice creams were being wolfed down, and I was grateful not to have to put up with the usual barrage of offensive nonsense about our players from the season-ticket holder next to me. For once, Tony the offensive electrician was in a good mood, and as I was chatting to him about how well Litton's midfield had been playing, the most peculiar thing happened.

I caught an eye.

Sitting two rows in front, and about ten seats away to my right, was Him.

We looked at each other.

I had only felt this way twice before: when Pretty Boy Pete first came down to training, and when I first noticed Toby some weeks before. The difference this time was that I knew hardly anything about Him. Only what I'd seen — a young guy, about my age, who came to the game with a couple of mates. He often wore sports gear — hoody tops, baseball cap, jeans, and white trainers, that sort of thing. He had short dark brown hair and piercing green eyes, with very white skin. That was all I knew for certain.

The first Saturday I saw Him it felt totally exciting, danger-ous, crazy. I was chatting about the game with Tony the offen-sive electrician, when I noticed Him looking back. We made eye contact, I looked away quickly, and then just as quickly looked back. He was still glancing at me. No smiles or anything, but a definite moment passed between us. After a good five sec-onds, one of his mates came back with a drink and they started chatting. I resumed my dull conversation.

I looked for Him at the final whistle, but he was out of the stadium pretty quick. Although I'd never felt that spark between me and another person at a footy game, I had seen dozens of guys who had sent my mind into confused mayhem, so I headed home thinking about Him but figuring that it was a one-off distraction, a moment of eye candy fun without words.

It turned out to be a whole lot more.

Two weeks later, I was back for our next home game — this time, an evening match. I kept a deliberate eye out for Him and sure enough he arrived a few minutes into the first half, his trusty mates at his side. I kept looking over, so much so that I nearly missed a Litton goal. But he wasn't reciprocating. Until halftime, that is. That's when I caught his eye again, and this time he smiled — he actually smiled! I felt scared, excited, and weird at the same time, which isn't a comfortable mix. I tried to smile back, but I think in retrospect the face I pulled probably made me look more as if I was in excruciating pain than that I was pleased to see Him. He had the most wonderful, face-brightening smile, and I was sure that the spark wasn't in my imagination. He nipped out and returned with a hot dog, then looked back up at me. I bottled it this time. Aware of the other fans seated around us, I couldn't maintain eye contact for fear of the obvious name-calling, so I looked away. This felt far more dangerous and "wrong" than meeting Toby's gaze in the lecture hall. At full-time he was out of the stadium sharpish again, and I was left with a train journey home during which I leant my head against the window and felt really, really happy. It wasn't long after Pod and Brenda had gone up north to their universities, and I was seeing less of Mikey. Toby had entered proceedings. In other words, it was a limbo period that I was floating through; a transitional patch between Lockham High and uni, between schoolboy and student, old friends and new.

I looked forward to the train journeys to and from the football. They gave me some time on my own to think about Him and fantasize about us having a conversation, sitting next to each other and cheering together when Alvaro Cruz knocked one into the back of the net. I wondered what his favorite color was, what music he liked, and whether he was a worker or a student. I built up a little creation in my mind; like a teenage Dr. Frankenstein, I took the good-looking face and lovely smile of this guy I had seen and created a whole character, including background and future. I decided his name was something like Scott or Luke, that he was indeed nineteen, and that he worked for his dad's firm — possibly decorating, possibly plumbing. He looked a bit like a plumber. I thought he probably attracted plenty of interest from girls, and that he was definitely no virgin. His favorite color was green and his favorite type of music was 1970s rock, like T-Rex and Mud. He loved beer and bitter, hated wine, and enjoyed a neat vodka on the rocks every now and then. He lived in Twickenham, South-West London, had supported Litton Park for as long as I had, and loved them through thick and thin as I had. We were very similar, Him and me, and I knew that it was only a matter of time before we would become great mates and start coming to matches together, enjoying a few drinks on a Saturday evening whilst analyzing the mistakes and triumphs of our beloved team.

I can't prove any of that is remotely true, and I've yet to sit next to Him at a game or enjoy a post-match tipple. But I continued to see Him throughout the season, and every time, without fail, we'd look at each other and smile, usually at halftime, occasionally before the game. I was sure he did it mainly when his mates weren't there, or when they were looking away. Once or twice, he looked back at me while Tony the offensive electrician was rabbiting on about something or other, and rolled his eyes in sympathy at me. I smiled back, and Tony looked around to see what was going on. Him was quick, though, and turned his head to avoid being caught out.

On one occasion, we were playing a League Cup game against the mighty Oldham Athletic. It was a freezing November night and our crowd totaled 3,500 — paltry and pathetic, even by Litton Park standards. My section of the seating was fairly empty, although Tony the offensive electrician was there of course, ready to hurl insults of every variety at both our players — who he thought were underachieving — and the Oldham lot. There were very few people in the seats around Him so I had a clear view of my mute friend for the entire game, which was so dull I used most of it as a chance to stare. I must have been watching the pitch that night for only a third of the match, the rest of my time dedicated to observing and hoping he'd turn around. I hate to sound pervy, but I really enjoyed watching. I looked forward to the football matches more for watching Him, noting his every reaction and facial expression that I could see, than for watching Litton. Every match he attended, without fail, we'd exchange a look, never longer than five seconds, never shorter than two (and yes, I timed them all). Then every train journey home my routine was rounded off with more fantasizing (I later decided he loved pizza and had a secret soft spot for musicals) and going over the look we had just exchanged a thousand times in my head.

As strange as it sounds, particularly given more recent events, I never once thought of anything sexual, intimate, or gay. It was all about Him, and nothing else. It was about stealing a glance that would keep me happy for days. Sure, in my head I wondered if we would become buddies, but I never once thought of him as anything other than a football mate. And at the same time, I longed for him to stare at me and smile with those glistening, glittering eyes. I was desperate for my fix of Him. On the few occasions he didn't make it to the game, I was distraught. I felt down. And then when he reappeared a few weeks later, I was back on cloud nine. He had that kind of effect on me. The rest of the time, while I was starting my new life at uni and playing for the Rangers, my mind was usually on other stuff. But for ninety minutes every other weekend, he had my attention. Immediately before and after the games, I would have his smile firmly embossed on my mind.

It sure made going to Litton Park a more pleasant experience. Our dismal run in the league last season saw us just a point above the relegation zone for much of the new year, and I was watching Him far more than the team, for which I felt guilty (the season ticket had been a birthday present from my mum and grandparents, and I was wasting it). I was reminded of the religious aspect to football; eyeing up another spectator is as sinful as flirting with a member of the congregation during mass. Having said that, my fear of being seen by another of the supporters faded as the season went on, although the danger aspect was definitely part of the fun. We introduced little nods to our silent duologues, and one afternoon I even had the nerve to walk right past Him and use the far exit instead of the one nearest me, as I went for a halftime toilet-seat analysis. This was around the same time I was beginning to be absolutely petrified and paralyzed by my feelings for Toby, so it may seem a little strange that I felt able to swagger past Him and even tilt my head slightly in his direction as I did so. But for me, this relationship was in my head. It was under my control and creation, and I was becoming fearless. I'm sure he got the message that day, because rather than disappearing hastily at the end of the game, he stood up, looked back at me, and gave me a little wink as he went on his way. A wink, for Christ's sake! That alone made my night.

One Saturday in April, just a couple of weeks before the end of the season, he arrived at the game with a cool new haircut. He had dyed a streak of hair blond, down the middle of his head. He looked striking and different. He got some stick from his mates, and some of the guys sitting behind him, but I could tell he was the kind of single-minded guy who didn't really care much what other people thought. Why, then, had he not ever made a move to come and speak to me? Admittedly I'd have probably frozen and clammed up, been at a complete loss for words, and made a twat out of myself, but I wondered why this guy — whose friends obviously respected and looked up to him, and who could dye his hair and walk around like a cowboy — why this guy couldn't speak to me. But somehow I liked it that he didn't. It kept me in control, in some strange way.

Still, with his new blond hair I found a novel mime technique to throw at him when he looked up at me in the halftime break. I rolled my eyes up as if to indicate my hair and gave him a tiny thumbs-up. I hadn't used my hands before. He responded with a broad smile and a rub of his hair. One of his mates noticed this and looked back, but I turned my head down to look engrossed in my match program. With the mate safely turned away, I returned to Him and smiled a little cheeky, side-of-my-mouth grin. He grinned back. That whole exchange felt really great, like he had kicked me up into the clouds. I was happy happy happy, even if I remained confused as to what the hell was going on in the rest of my life, particularly as regards Pretty Boy and, of course, Toby, whose eye I also kept catching. But there were none of these little games with Toby. I felt a buzz whizz through me at every Litton game. The team had turned around their fortune and were now cruising for a top twelve finish in the league, which was a predictable — but welcome — relief.

I arrived deliberately early for the last match of the season, thinking that maybe Him would have the same plan and we could share some quality mime. It was a little ridiculous how I had become the silent movie star of the Litton Park terraces; I spent train journeys considering what moves to try out next time, and rehearsed them, which led to strange looks from the other commuters. Still, it made me wonder how on earth sign language worked, and how tricky it must be to differentiate between certain gestures.

I took my seat in the stadium at about 2:15 P.M., a good forty-five minutes before kickoff. I read the program, as usual full of dull and obvious comments from the club captain and coach, and lots of adverts for products most football fans wouldn't have any interest in. And then, at 2:25 P.M. precisely, in walked Him, by himself. He approached his seat, stood by it, and looked up at me. I looked at Him. Ten seconds. Ten whole seconds — a new staring record! We smiled at each other — I'm not sure how I looked, probably like a grinning maniac about to pour petrol over his family and fire a flamethrower — but I know *he* looked very flirtatious. Maybe because the terrace was still fairly empty, maybe because it was the last game for a few months, or maybe because he had new blond hair and felt particularly cocky — I don't really know why — but a newfound bravery had overcome Him, and it spread to me. After our ten-second stare, he opened up his program and leafed through it, while I did the same. We kept looking up at exactly the same time, and after a few of these coincidental looks, we both burst out laughing. Tony the offensive electrician gave me a funny stare. But still no words, and no suggestion that there would be. Regardless, I loved every minute. It was like we were great, great friends, and I felt a lot of the stuff you feel when you're with good friends — relaxed, contented, a little open. The fact we'd never spoken didn't matter to me, nor apparently to Him. He was my silent friend.

Despite having met Toby, and having opened up to him with the sort of conversation I would never have dreamed myself capable of, Him was — and still is — an important part of my life. He was a different type of friend. He couldn't disappoint or offend me, despise or upset me. He was whatever I wanted him to be.

CHAPTER 7

LONG, HOT SUMMER DAYS

In the week after my first official get-together with Toby, he and I decided to meet up again. It wasn't anywhere near as eventful an occasion, however. Whiling away a Wednesday watching the most addictive and dire daytime TV lifestyle programs, I texted Toby and suggested we "hook up for coffee." I don't actually drink coffee, but it's a useful expression, and after the explosion of sandwich and espresso shops in the late 1990s, "going for a coffee" has become a new British pastime. Toby drank a sophisticated latte while I sipped orange juice. We'd already covered a lot of the get-to-know-you heavy stuff, so this was a pleasant antidote. We just chilled, talked about the history degree, swapped stories of eccentric and drunken academics, and finished off with a game of Frisbee in the famous park. It was actually quite chilly, but the sun was out and so, being Britain, everybody jumped into shorts and sleeveless tops, exposing deathly pale limbs. Luckily, Toby and I had opted for far more sensible clothing.

It felt so easy. Our second *occasion* together lasted only a few hours, but I was so glad we met and enjoyed every single minute of the time we shared. As liberating and enjoyable as the big chat was, simply doing nothing together felt just as important.

Two days later, on the Friday, Brenda, Pod, and I had forgone our usual drinking session for a visit to the cinema. I never felt like a third wheel when I was out with them. Maybe it's because I'd known them so long, or because they felt sorry for me being single for so long, but they never seemed to mind me being with them. Pod nearly got us thrown out of the local multiplex before the film even started when he was caught smuggling in contraband: a bottle of Coke and a packet of chocolates he'd bought at the newsagents. We saw a romantic comedy, an experience spoilt somewhat by a bunch of kids in the rows behind laughing whenever any of the characters said "shit," "piss," or "dick." Fortunately, it didn't matter since the corny film was a bag of shite. These so-called "chick flicks" are so predictable. The beautiful boy and girl always end the movie together, so why they bother going through all these near break-ups and misunderstandings beats me. We're not stupid. We know they're going to live happily ever after. If these movies would just cut to the final scene after the third, we could all save some time.

Bored out of her undergraduate skull, Brenda phoned me on the Saturday morning and invited me to go window-shopping. She was determined to find a funky T-shirt similar to the one worn by Jennifer, the main character in the rom-com. So she and I hit the nearby shopping town of Kingston early — about ten A.M. — and by 10:30 I remembered why I so disliked shopping with girls, even Brenda. The indecisiveness. The contemplation. The "does it match what I already own?" The general fannying about. It's intolerable. She said Pod was useless at giving advice on clothes and shoes, when in fact I knew that he pretended to be inept just so that he could skive off shopping with her. It was an arduous experience, but once she'd found a tiger-print T-shirt that vaguely resembled the one from the movie, I persuaded her to come to the ice cream shop with me. We bought three large scoopfuls each and went on a walk through a small park. All around us there were mad shoppers, pacing in crazy rushes as the world around them seemed to hardly move at all. Next to the park, the church still stood, its bells ominously striking twelve, and the early afternoon sun blazed on top of us with the power of an open-doored oven.

Long, hot summer days always brought back memories of my childhood; the July/August holidays were always the significant ones, when the most growing up was done. This year would be no different, even though I was a bit older. The reason I philosophized in the brief moments of silence as we walked round the park is that this was an important moment for me. It felt like the first time I could reconcile the two main elements of my life — my past and my present, both formed by experiences based in the same town. I hadn't moved on to new geographical pastures like Brenda and Pod, but walking around town with Brenda, it hit me just how much I was changing. The town was the same, but it seemed different because *I* felt different. I hadn't spent any time alone with Brenda for ages, certainly not since I'd started having all these confusions. But I knew she knew there was something going on.

Sometimes I wonder if our lives are more like the movies than the movies. Things happen that you just couldn't make up — things so corny even the chick flick wouldn't have gotten away with them. There we were, strolling along, when someone came up from behind me, put his hands over my eyes, and said, "Guess who?" I pulled his hands away and turned to see Toby grinning at me. He was wearing his white factory overall with *Rotheray Biscuits* embroidered on the front. I was totally taken aback, as usual. And the way my heart started beating, you'd have thought I'd just run the London Marathon. After a short while, he helped me out:

"Nice to see you too, Sam. . . ."

"Er . . . sorry," I blurted. "Nice to see you. Toby, this is Brenda."

"Pleased to meet you," she said, and he answered with something similar.

"Sam's told me a lot about you. Says you've been friends a while," he said.

"Ten years," said Brenda. "I've put up with the mong for a decade."

Toby laughed, then made his excuses about being late for work and left. I was still dumbstruck, not least because I was worrying about the impression I gave him — whether I looked cool or totally ruffled. I caught Brenda smiling at me in that "I know what you're thinking" kind of way.

"Quite fit, isn't he?" she said. I wasn't ready to discuss the cuteness of boys with her yet.

"I wouldn't know. I don't fancy him, you know. We're just very good friends."

"Just like you didn't fancy Josh, right?"

"Oi," I said, telling her off for knowing me so well. "Brenda, I don't fancy Toby, all right?"

"And what if he fancies you?"

"Why? What did you notice?"

"I see. . . ." She smiled.

"See what?"

"Well, he *does* fancy you. Body language." And she showed me an example of negative body language (arms folded) followed by the kind of lingering look that she said Toby was giving me (positive). To this day I still think she was just stirring, provoking me to admit my feelings. She couldn't have honestly believed he fancied me, but then Toby's sexual energy confused a lot of people. Some people have that energy, some people don't (I most certainly don't). But it's a weird thing, because you kind of perspire it, and people instantly think you fancy them, or instantly fancy you, which can be a good thing or a nightmare.

"So what are you going to do about it?" she asked me.

"I'm not going to do anything about it, Brenda, because I don't feel sexually for him. I like him a lot as a friend."

"Ever imagined him naked?"

I couldn't believe she was being so unashamedly candid. And in public too. I glanced about to see if any young scallies were listening, ready to start spitting at me and shouting, "Oi, bum boy!"

"God, how can you ask that?" I exclaimed furiously.

She continued, as calm as the day was sunny, "Because if you have, then you know it's probably more than just good friends."

"But is it? I mean, can you be sure?"

I was making a right bodge job of this. Even if I didn't fancy him, she wouldn't believe me now. She put a hand on mine.

"Sam, you think too much. Just chill out, go with your gut."

"My gut's confusing." My first one hundred percent honest answer of the day, apart from when I told her the beige-and-orange jeans she was considering buying were fucking dire.

"What's going on, Brenda?" I stopped and looked ground-ward, scared that making eye contact would render me even more vulnerable.

She suddenly turned very serious, and stopped teasing.

"You're being honest," she said, and at once I knew she'd figured it out. Not only that she knew, but that she understood. That I could say what I liked, because Brenda had been waiting for this day since the Josh incident, or even earlier. She knew I had issues, and this was the time, at last, to discuss them. I felt more at ease, and slumped into a bench we'd come to. Brenda sat next to me, facing me, waiting for me.

"Maybe things were easier when I wasn't being honest," I started, still finding it hard to put into words what I was think-ing, still finding it hard to look at her. "You're just a friend, right? So why aren't I close to any bloke in the way I'm close to you?" This question adequately summed up my feelings. I was by no means sure I wanted sex with a boy, but beer and hand-shakes wouldn't do either. I wanted something more, some-thing closer.

"I don't know, Sam. But there's nothing stopping you being close to a guy, if you want to be," she said.

"Yeah, there is."

"For instance?"

"For instance . . . the small matter of being in the football team. This isn't Manchester uni, Brenda."

"Sorry. But you shouldn't feel pressure. If people have a problem with you, they're not worth knowing. You're my best friend, and you're the dog's bollocks as far as I'm concerned."

She's so special. I love Brenda. I had been thinking of asking her for some time, and I felt relaxed enough to just come out with it —

"You heard of Bliss?"

"Course I have. Wanna go?"

"Thought we could. Just give it a try. Nothing more."

"Next week sometime?"

"Thanks, Brends," I said, putting a hand on hers. "Have you ever thought you might be a closet fag hag?"

She went bananas. "I am not a fag hag! How dare you? I'm not enough of a fucked-up recluse to be a fag hag. I hate Marilyn Monroe. And I'd never wear glitter. Sod off, Smith."

I apologized and she smiled at me. There was a lengthy pause. She was giving me room and time to speak. I looked at her for the first time.

"I tell you what really fucks me off. Why is it always assumed I'm a good heterosexual boy? Since I was five years old it's been 'Have you got a girlfriend yet?' or 'I bet you'll stun the girls in that outfit, Sam.' But nobody stops to think 'What if he's not just into girls?' No one ever assumes a kid could be anything other than straight. And that pisses me off."

"You know, I'd never thought of that before."

"Not many people have," I said. "The pressure's put on you when you're a toddler to make other people happy, to live up to their expectations."

I leaned forward and began playing with my hair — a nervous habit.

"I definitely need a shag. It'll get things out of my system," I said.

"No, a shag won't help," she said immediately. "Take it from me, Sam, I lost it to someone else's boyfriend. In a toilet cubicle." I knew about this, but we hadn't talked about it for years. Brenda lost it at age fifteen to John Field, a good-looking guy in the year above us at school. It messed her up bad at the time. "He fucked me then fucked off," she continued. "I'll never forget that feeling. Slaggish, guilty, used. I'd . . . I'd give anything to go back. You can't build a relationship on sex."

She was absolutely right. Sex needn't be all that important; it certainly isn't worth getting very hung up about. But somehow it managed to get me thinking and worrying even more. Can you be gay if you don't touch each other's knobs? Can you be in a straight relationship if you don't shag each other? My conclusion on the park bench was of course you can. As well as being a meaningless bit of fun, sex is an expression of love, as is writing a poem, or buying a bunch of flowers, or cooking a plush meal. Sex doesn't mean love. So maybe that was what I was — a celibate multisexual. But then, I thought, given the chance, I'd be quite good at sex. I had ideas, imagination, a willingness to experiment and try most things twice. It was, however, refreshing to find out that someone in a long relationship thought sex wasn't all that important. It made me feel less pressured to identify my feelings.

As we were both being so open, I decided to ask how things were going with Pod. I said he'd been talking a lot of shite lately, which I thought was harsh but fair.

"You don't know him like I do . . . when we're alone, he's so different," she vouched. "He's sensitive and kind." I looked disbelievingly at her. "I mean it. It's only booze that turns him into King of the Dickheads." She looked down and fidgeted with her fingers. "But . . . I'd be lying if I said I hadn't thought about calling last orders. I've found a side to him I wish I hadn't. Still, at least I'm getting to know Pod now."

"Give us a hug," I demanded, standing up. And she did. And it felt so warm and good — the sun was shining on my back and I felt lucky. Lucky to have such a good friend, and lucky that I was at last able to talk to someone. A lot of people probably didn't have that.

"You're happy, though?" I asked her.

"Happier than most. You?"

"Course not."

She seemed surprised. We hugged again.

"But luckier than most," I said softly into her ear.

CHAPTER 8

"OUR AUNT — SHE DON'T WANNA KNOW, SHE SAYS, 'WHAT WILL THE NEIGHBORS THINK?'" — MADNESS

Two days later, on a humid Monday evening, Toby attended his first Rangers training session. Immediately after, I had no option but to sit in the park toilet again. I was buzzing with thoughts and worries, and simply had to sit down, calm down, and take everything in. It all happened so quickly, but I recalled with a bit of horror how the bizarre events unfolded.

The first thing that struck me was how good a footballer he was. He was quick, a cunning dribbler, with an awesome left foot. His heading skills left a lot to be desired, and he seemed quite nervous, but given that this was his first time with the Rangers, and he hadn't played football at all for some time, it was an excellent performance.

Toby's arrival was no big deal. Players come and go every week — students who want to get fit quick might come for a couple of months then never reappear; older men who think they can hack the pace frequently disappear; friends and siblings of the regulars often come down for a session and maybe even a game or two before calling it quits. Nobody gave Toby a second look. But it wasn't long before the others noticed he was no ordinary addition to the squad.

His stare was lingering — mainly on Pretty Boy, I noticed, but also on one or two of the others. Pretty Boy was his usual cool James Dean-esque self, shooting a look back at Toby every now and then. The lads wore puzzled expressions as they witnessed Toby's roving eye.

He was very cheery and friendly from the get-go, making jokes and even teasing me on a couple of crappy shots on goal I'd tried. Trevor, who during shooting practice once again proved he couldn't hit a horse's arse with a telegraph pole, came in for some mild mocking from Laid Back, which Toby laughed along with heartily. Trevor, his sweaty hair whipping his forehead, huffed and puffed and looked bitterly at Laid Back, who took to trying shots on goal whilst smoking. This sort of behavior is totally unacceptable, but he was the only left back we had, so Harry couldn't upset him.

The first overt moment of Toby's unstraightness came during team sprinting, when he turned to me and said, "Not the cutest team in the world. You should ask for a free transfer."

I was shocked into silence. I just ran faster, trying to get away from him. What did he think he was doing, talking about cute footy teams in front of the lads? I wondered if Toby was naive, stupid, or just completely bonkers. I was fairly certain that Chopper Chubby heard this remark, as he kept looking at me and Toby with a funny eye for the rest of the session. I was seriously regretting my suggestion that Toby join the Rangers and quickly became desperate for training to end. I felt drained and groggy, more out of the fear that had overtaken me than anything else. I was just dreading the moment Toby made another telltale remark, as I knew he would. He didn't seem to care that I was an integral part of this team, and that any suggestion of improper behavior would probably lead to my dismissal.

This training session seemed to go on forever. I was a nervous wreck by the time Morph terminated things by throwing a temper tantrum. He was always high-strung and unreasonable, but an actual tantrum was rare. Harry had berated us during the football tennis game with a shout of "Now that was bloody rubbish, start again!" This was bad news. Football tennis took ages, because we played it like a proper tennis match — 15–love, 30–love, deuce, etc.

Morph was usually given a whistle, though if he ever so much as thought about using it he was chastised by his superior. On this occasion, however, Morph had left his whistle at home, and had spent most of the session asking Harry to borrow his. Harry kept fobbing him off, disinterested in the petty tools of management politics, since the petty tool was his. Harry eventually handed it over, granting permission for Morph to blow full-time on the training match, but as Morph blew, he also covered the whistle's blow-gap with his finger, muting any noise it might have made. He looked absolutely downtrodden before throwing the whistle onto the grass and stamping on it repeatedly with his right foot in a fit of pure rage. Harry, who was once a bouncer in a cheesy nightclub, linked his arms into Morph's and pulled him away from the whistle, ordering calm. They looked ridiculous — like a bad version of Laurel and Hardy.

Morph shouted at us, "Game over. Drill number one!"

I felt relieved that it was nearly all over. Toby had behaved himself for all of ten minutes and, despite the shifty stares, I was convinced Chopper, Mikey, and Laid Back were giving me, I knew that harmony would soon be restored.

We all gathered in two lines for drill number one, a pointless waste of time that involved jumping on one another's backs, crawling through one another's legs, and then clapping five times like some sort of flamenco dancer. Toby found it funny. I'd never really thought about it, but I guess the sight of eleven young men in shorts bending over and crawling through one another's legs must have appeared quite odd to an outsider.

The drill completed, we all started warming down, taking boots off, and examining pustules and blisters, while Harry and Morph held their traditional post-training briefing, during which Harry told Morph what he thought and Morph agreed. As usual, Pretty Boy disappeared quick. I avoided eye contact with anybody as best I could. By now, I was exhausted.

"Pretty Boy says it's still hurting. Potential team crisis," Morph informed Harry, excited at the prospect of somebody other than him having a serious problem to deal with. Harry called for Toby, and I moved closer as I stretched in order to get within earshot. "Pretty Boy Pete has had —" Harry started.

"Why *is* he called Pretty Boy Pete?" Toby interrupted.

A pause. I think Toby was trying to get one of them to explain how Pete was a dashingly handsome young man, but instead —

"Because he *is* a Pretty Boy —" started Harry.

"— and his name is Pete," concluded Morph.

Toby replied quick as a flash:

"He's not that pretty."

94

Harry's face wore a look of unbridled horror.

"What?" he demanded.

"Well, I've seen prettier."

Morph looked at Harry, at a loss. Was this a member of the Rangers saying he'd seen prettier boys? Surely not! Harry took the *ignore it, and it'll go away* approach. Mikey stopped packing his kit bag and just stared at Toby, a look of total confusion on his face. Chopper Chubby's narrow, suspicious eyes focused on the new boy too. I was beginning to sweat.

"Yeah, well . . . his hamstring's looking dodge," Harry continued. "I want you to try for us at left mid, but you've got to concentrate on your ball control."

"Ball control's my speciality," Toby cheeked. Chopper gave Laid Back a look. My shirt was, by now, drenched and I was nervously picking tiny pieces of dry summer mud out of my boots.

"What?" said Harry, sternly.

"Nothing," Toby replied.

I think Harry was having second thoughts about his offer. I was on the verge of exploding with embarrassment. Toby was outing himself and, by default, me.

"What's your favored position?" asked Morph, and I could see where this one was going. Toby grinned.

"My favored position, since you ask, is in the hole."

This was the straw that broke Harry's back. Irreverent humor was bad enough, but innuendo? Beyond the pale. His voice turned all gravelly and threatening, sounding a bit like a cheap East End gangster.

"You being funny?"

"Funny?"

"I asked you where you like to play on the pitch," explained Harry, still resembling a London Godfather.

"I told you, in the hole," said Toby.

Morph didn't get it. "The hole? The hole? Where's the hole? Could be anywhere, couldn't it? Specify!"

"Between midfield and attack, the hole," explained Toby, and he wasn't wrong — the hole was a position made popular by teams in Italy.

Harry told Toby to warm down, and crouched by me as I took my boots off. Morph crouched behind him, annoyingly. I knew I'd be interrogated, and Harry pulled no punches.

"This . . . friend. Quite nifty on his feet . . ."

"Quite useful in the air," pitched in Morph. For once, I agreed.

"Yeah, showed me up a bit, I reckon," I said.

"Yes, he did," said Morph, which wasn't what I expected.

"Leave tactical opinions to me, please," said Harry. "He around a lot, is he?"

"He's staying for the summer. Working at the biscuit factory," I explained, slightly wary of what was to come. Harry seemed to be beating about the bush a bit.

"Is he now? Round for the Summer Cup, then?" asked the gaffer. I answered in the affirmative. Then came the question Harry was dying to ask.

"Exactly how much of a friend is he?"

"What do you mean?" I asked, keeping my eyes on the ground.

"Well . . . he seemed quite similar," said Harry.

"Quite gentle," added Morph.

"I just know him quite well, that's all. We do the same subject."

Harry got back to business. "Know him well enough to convince him to play left mid? On a trial period, mind."

I was a bit taken aback. I knew we were short on left-footed players, but he'd only played one training session, and he was already being considered for the first team. Of course I could convince him to play, although I wasn't sure, in light of Toby's cheekiness, that this was the best idea for me personally.

"We want him in, we think he's great!" squealed Morph.

"Morph! Remember what I told you about you annoying me, about talking out of turn? Well, you're doing it now."

"I'm sorry," began Morph, "but I was just trying to exercise my right. It's difficult. I mean I've got to raise my self-esteem, the whole point of the counseling —"

"Morph — I repeat: You're doing it now."

I offered to have a word with Toby about trialing. But I was far more concerned with finding out what Toby had revealed about personal matters.

"Has he told you anything?" I asked. "Like, about himself?"

Harry leaned in. He had an annoying smirk on the left side of his mouth. Morph looked very excited as he said —

"Oh yes, he's told us all about the —"

"Morph! Bloody hell!" shouted Harry, getting up to leave. What he said next filled me with terror.

"He's told us he's . . . gentle. Know what I mean?"

And with that he and Morph were off, gathering all the balls and cones. Most of the team had gone by now too, apart from Trevor, who was fruitlessly practicing shots by himself, and

Toby, who was doing keep-ups with a ball. I grabbed him by the arm.

"Are you mad?" I asked, although it was meant to be rhetorical.

"Frequently," he said. He clearly wasn't getting my drift.

"I mean, it's all very cool, Toby, all very open-minded and la-di-da, but this is football!"

"Well, it's about time it caught up with the rest of the world," he said, as casually as could be.

"You can't go telling football coaches you're into boys. You'll be telling your dad next."

"Not bloody likely." A moment of sincere sensitivity amid all the cocky confidence. He could be human after all. But I was worried, and more than somewhat.

"People will talk. About me."

"Oh, excuse me for not thinking," he said, catching the ball in his hands. But I had a point; it was me who introduced him to the team, and I certainly didn't expect him to sail quite so close to the wind at his first training session. It was downright disrespectful.

"Look, he asked if I had a girlfriend," Toby explained. "I said no but that I wasn't fussy about what I chose. *Anything on two legs* was my exact expression. I laughed. He just looked at me like I was mad."

Toby — that's Toby, the guy *I* had brought along to football training — told Harry, the coach of a football team, that he wasn't fussy about what he chose. I was filled with that horrible tingly feeling all over, that sensation mix of embarrassment and fear. Did he realize the potential implications of his revelation? I told him he was fucking mad, to which he replied:

"I'm sorry to be an embarrassment."

This hit me. I'd obviously hurt him, which probably meant he cared, which in turn meant he truly considered me a close friend. Somehow, all those thoughts passed through my mind in a couple of seconds. I guess I *was* being a tad selfish.

"No . . . no, don't be sorry. You're right. It's great. I mean, this could be great. He wants you to try out for the Cup game despite what you said. Harry might just be a tolerant bastard after all. You're opening doors, Toby," I said, not really convinced by a word of it.

He perked up. "Shall we try our luck, then? With Harry?" He laughed and threw the ball at me. I caught it. This was more like the Toby I knew.

"Fuck off! I still wanna have my balls in the morning," I joked, although I guess deep down I knew that any bloke who made a pass on Harry would be signing his own death warrant. I chucked the ball at Toby.

"You'll still have your balls," he said, kind of staring at me in a strange daze. He threw the ball back, taking a step towards me.

"You sure of that?" I asked, feeling slightly taken in by his stare. Our eyes were now locked. It felt weird, but good. I hurled the ball and took a step closer. We were two boys, in football kit, in public, in a park, staring each other in the eyes and moving closer.

"Certain," he said.

I went to grab the ball back but he swung it round behind his back and just stayed staring at me. Checkmate.

"I like certain."

That was all I could think of to say. It was only then that I fully realized how bright his brown eyes were. I was spellbound, and could have stared at them all day. The sexual tension was unbearable. Yet I didn't feel at any moment as if either of us was going to make a move. It was strange, as if we were excited by the stare and only the stare. After a few seconds of silence — which felt like minutes — Toby interrupted our torpor.

"Well, I should go," he said.

"Yeah, me too. I need the toilet." Made perfect sense to me — I needed time to reflect. But I can understand that to anybody else, it would seem an insane thing to say at a moment like this. Toby looked bewildered.

"Nothing," I said, avoiding any attempt at an explanation. "See ya, then. . . ."

Toby walked off. I watched him go, half expecting him to turn around and wave or wink or something, but he didn't. I ran into the toilet, which was completely empty, sat myself down, locked the cubicle door, and held my head in my hands. For some inexplicable reason, I cried a bit. After a few minutes, and some very rough-surfaced toilet paper to wipe my tears, I composed myself. I hate crying, but I'm not very good at controlling myself. I thought about being twelve and having sleepover parties, and cried even more. I was desperate to go back. But the problems still had to be confronted, so after I'd awoken from my nostalgia trip, I assessed the facts.

Harry definitely sniffed a rat. Or a fruit, I should say. I believed this could present several problems, not least relentless teasing on the pitch and possible expulsion from the Rangers. I reasoned that the whole team would be calling me "bum bandit" by the end of the next training session. I wondered if this was an English thing, or if it's difficult to be yourself anywhere in the world. If we lived somewhere else, would it be a problem to get close to your male friends?

I decided there was a place where I could be myself, where there were no prerequisites as to how people should behave: PetShopBoyLand (near Finland, a tiny state with big ambitions), where all blokes would be as cozy as girls. Because over there, blokes pecked on the cheek when they met and held hands in public because they wanted to, because they were friends. In PetShopBoyLand, I reckoned, I might meet a bloke. An ordinary bloke. A bloke who didn't want to start a fight. A bloke who talked, and wasn't embarrassed to talk, or scared to admit liking bubble baths and plucking his eyebrows. A bloke who didn't say, "Ooh . . . can I watch?" when he met a lesbian couple, who didn't pretend to be able to do an hour's car journey in forty minutes to prove his manliness. A bloke who didn't lie about how many pints it took to get him pissed. A bloke who admitted to still having his teddy bear and using skin moisturizer. But PetShopBoyLand was far away, and all flights had been canceled.

I pulled the toilet chain.

CHAPTER 9

"WE WERE IN LONDON. TELL IT LIKE IT IS."
— PET SHOP BOYS

Perhaps feeling guilty after his rather open display at the training session, or perhaps because he had some cunning ulterior motive, Toby invited me to go up to London with him for the day. It was a Thursday, a few days after the Rangers nightmare.

I jumped at the chance. Where better than London to find anonymity and seclusion? Caught within the bustle of people and vehicles, shops and offices, Toby and I could slide about without anyone caring in the slightest. Back home, a sneeze in the Church and Abbey would make the local newspapers.

London always seemed to me to be a city that did not judge, where you could go about your business without fear of scrutiny or criticism. It is the human zoo, the walk-through safari park in which the people are both exhibits and spectators. It also serves as the magnet of England, drawing in people from all over the planet, many of whom never leave. Quite why, I had never understood, but then my experiences had been limited to the parts of London which seemed to be inhabited purely by drunken Home Counties youths. Toby had mentioned how he and his ex-boyfriend Paul used to visit Soho when they were together. It was the only place they could truly be themselves without fear of being queer-bashed.

But whilst the city serves as a good hiding place to be ignored and blanked and generally treated as though invisible, it is also the biggest show in the land. Some walk down the streets like models on a catwalk, desperate for their style to be noted. Some live their London lives as though they are on the stage, vying for the audience's attention.

But the vast majority just seem to get on with their lot and spend most of the time avoiding eye contact — or any type of contact — with other people. The one thing I always noticed as a kid when mum took me to see the Regent's Street Christmas lights, or the Science Museum, or whatever, was the pace of the place. London was — and remains — a city operating in fifth gear, with only occasional rest in fourth, and no mercy for those who choose to ride in third. There is a sense of life-threatening urgency, as if the slightest letup in pace would lead to mass collapse. The city is not famous for qualities of generosity or selflessness, although apparently during the war Londoners all clubbed together with the indomitable British spirit, or something. This is certainly not the case now. I have never felt especially comfortable in London, although on this occasion, the prospect of not being in Surbiton, where I recognized so many people, was quite appealing.

I suppose the upshot was that I expected London to offer me the opportunity to be myself without feeling that constant pressure and intimidation.

As well as being the perfect location for Toby and I to explore each other, our day out was also a chance to explore the big city. Toby assured me he knew some "cool places to go," having "experienced" London when he was a schoolkid in Maidstone, and more recently whilst living in Surbiton. Toby went into town a little earlier than me to try to find some books he needed for college, and I came up later. We met at noon, underneath the big and famous clock in Waterloo train station. Unfortunately, the grand, imposing clock has lost some of its mysticism and romance since the station managers decided to build numerous shops and information boards around it. It is now hidden in a sea of unnecessary stores selling unnecessary things to people like me who, while waiting for a train, decide that the most essential and urgent thing in the world to purchase is a turquoise dolphin paper-and-envelope box set.

So we met underneath the clock, and I was fifteen minutes late owing to signal failure at Vauxhall, which is a far better excuse than one I heard some weeks ago — "Sorry we're running late, but the train behind us is going slowly."

I saw Toby approach with a cup of hot tea in his hand, and I started to feel nervous again, like the first time I met him. Although we hadn't started yet, the day was beginning to resemble a first real date. The last time we'd been together, there was such a powerful charge between us that I was totally unsure of what to expect from our excursion. Just seeing him approach made me all charged up again. He was wearing a short-sleeve, navy blue shirt, with dark blue jeans and his bright skater trainers. He looked boss. I had taken a while to decide what to wear, worrying myself about what would and wouldn't impress him. I settled on a plain white T-shirt, baggy combats, and trainers. As

I bundled out of the front door, my mum tried to thrust a jumper on me in case the weather turned, but, as ever, I ignored her.

Toby and I said our hellos, I apologized for my lateness, and then I nearly collapsed.

It was Him.

Standing amid a group of geezers outside one of the fast-food restaurants on the concourse, his back half turned towards me, but with the distinctive remnants of the dyed blond streak, I was convinced it was Him from Litton Park. There must have been around ten others with him, all very tough, straight-looking blokes. I froze and stared, but before I could get a good look, they had disappeared. Toby was shaking me by the shoulders.

"Sam? Sam!" he shouted, breaking me out of my catatonia.

I made some fumbling excuse about being tired and thinking I had seen an old friend, which Toby half believed.

It was definitely Him. My curiosity was now at fever pitch. I didn't just want to know more — I *needed* to. It's hard to explain quite why, given that I'd never even met the guy. However, I was determined not to spoil my big day with Toby, and so I tried to put Him to the side of my mind, if not the back, and concentrate on having a good time.

We headed off in the direction of the South Bank, our first destination on this whistle-stop tour of the capital. It being a bright and clear day, Toby thought it was a perfect opportunity to venture up the London Eye, the famous landmark along the River Thames. Essentially a gigantic Ferris wheel, this tall device is made up of several glass-paneled booths that rotate slowly in a complete circle from which, when you reach the top, you can see most of the city. Toby had been once before, and assured me the spectacular views would be worth the hour-long queue (which actually turned out to be an hour and a half). I didn't mind, though. It gave us a chance to chat about . . . well, about nothing much really. We managed to fill over an hour with conversations about bad TV, kids' TV, good TV, reality TV, and even some interesting topics. The point is, it all felt effortless, and easy, and chilled, and I felt happy just to be with him. There was a slightly different vibe to our time together that day, however. Toby seemed to be smiling a lot more. In turn, I smiled back. He wasn't grinning in a happy-clapper kind of way; it looked more like the type of smile you pull when you're slightly embarrassed, or confident, or pleased to see someone. Also, I could have sworn he was touching me more — never in a sexual way, just the odd arm-grab, or pat on the back. Whenever we walked side by side, our shoulders seemed to brush against each other. But I concluded that nothing new was going on; it was just that, after the tension down at the park, I was being ultra-observant.

The Eye was, as my new friend predicted, amazing. We were in a booth with a bunch of German tourists. One of them looked a bit like Judy from Tom's satellite porn collection; Toby couldn't understand why I was grinning like a Cheshire cat as we reached the top of the wheel and could see across London and into the Home Counties. The view was awesome. Everything seemed so much smaller, and suddenly London felt less daunting, less threatening. It was an excellent, disarming start to our day. Above all, it was the kind of experience I wanted to share with someone special. Thanks to Toby, I had.

We got on the Underground at Waterloo and, after a change of line, arrived at the next location on Toby's carefully planned list: Regent's Park. I had never been to this sprawling slab of central London greenery before, or the London Zoo, which sat inside. Toby said he hated zoos and I agreed, more to impress him than anything else. I had never given zoo ethics much thought. We grabbed a sandwich and sat on a bench, eating in the sun, watching an impromptu game of football. I noticed how many different nationalities seemed to be represented in the game — there were several Spanish speakers, a couple of French, and the odd Italian and West Indian. Not quite the Surbiton Rangers.

It was about 2:30 and the sun was warming my face, as well as probably doing my skin a lot of damage.

"What d'you think so far?" Toby asked me.

"Yeah, wicked," I replied, a little hesitantly.

"Ever been to Camden Town?"

"No, but I heard about it. There's a big market there, right?"

"Let's go," he said, grabbing my wrist and whisking me back underground. We could have walked, but why bother when you can take a stuffy, baking-hot, mouse-infested public transport system that leaves you feeling irritable and dirty? Using the Tube that day made me grateful I didn't have to get on the bloody thing every day.

We arrived at Camden Town station, which was absolutely heaving with people. The heat was stifling and the humidity made the clothes stick to my skin. I checked my T-shirt hadn't gone see-through. A rotund commuter was involved in a hearty row with a ticket inspector at the main exit gate, while we sauntered out into the bustling Camden High Street.

The expression "all human life is here" sprang to mind immediately.

I was completely taken aback, struggling to play it cool in front of Toby. The place was crawling with weirdos and misfits, vagrants and wanna-bes. There was a carnival-like atmosphere, and I felt a little intimidated and slightly uneasy with the surroundings, which leant themselves more to a gangster movie than a fiesta. Behind the happy, sun-kissed facade, I wondered if there lurked sinister forces ready to pounce. It was probably the most intriguing, contradictory, and odd atmosphere I had ever encountered. Having Toby with me, and all the mind games he brought with him, played a big part in this. But I found myself strangely attracted to the vibe, and I liked the chaos, which at times seemed lawless; walking down the manic High Street, we were offered marijuana three times, pills twice, and even an air rifle.

Black, white, and Asian mixed easily. Bottle-blonds and real blonds mingled with punks and pensioners. Goths in traditional dark makeup and black clothes were scattered about everywhere — I'd never seen so many in one place. Toby led me in the direction of the Lock, and on the walk down we passed countless cheap clothes and record stores, selling things that were so unfashionable they had become fashionable again. There were several benches along the High Street on which old dossers sat, sipping extra-strong cider from plastic bottles, their savage-looking dogs occasionally growling at passersby. I noticed the strange similarity between the dogs' features and those of their weather-beaten, embittered owners.

Teenagers with Nirvana T-shirts wandered among middle-aged hippies and bent-backed wrinklies buying their weekend groceries. The air was filled with a heavy, dense stink of fried steak and incense. The noise was a bizarre mix of the everyday and the outright mad; the ever-present growl and horns of traffic morphed with the strained sounds of a busking violinist. As we walked on, the violin was replaced by a tweeting bird cry. The source of the authentic-sounding shrill was not a sparrow or a sandpiper, but a wooden instrument a blind man was selling for peanuts. A thumping bass and treble-heavy guitar riff suggested a band was playing in a pub somewhere close.

There was food all around too. Restaurants, cafes, pubs, street vendors with hot-dog and pizza carts — the choice was vast and, it seemed to me, mostly awful. We approached the marketplace, which was, as Toby had warned me, packed full of people and stalls, some dodgy, some OK. Plenty of clothes, lots of CDs (many of them bootlegs and pirate copies) as well as some stalls selling useless bric-a-brac.

A buxom gothic woman offered me a temporary tattoo.

"I'll write what you like on it . . . Peace, Mum, your girlfriend's name. . . ."

I looked at her and politely declined, while Toby pitched in with one of his annoying, sarcastic comments:

"Will you write my name on his arm?"

She smiled and turned her attentions to the next potential customer. I felt my customary uncomfortable sensations, and walked briskly on to a clothes stall specializing in the latest Bangladeshi trends.

We grabbed some ice creams from a shifty-looking man with dirty fingernails. It's impossible to eat an ice cream without licking, and it's impossible to lick without thinking of something lewd. I kept looking at Toby as he worked on his vanilla, and I caught him watching me as I gorged on my chocolate. At one point, we laughed out loud watching each other lick. The giggle broke the tension, ensuring the moment wasn't a repeat of the park episode a few nights previously.

"Wanna try?" Toby offered.

I must have looked like a right dufus. I politely declined, shuffled embarrassedly on the spot, then smiled. But this wasn't a happy, confident, or pleased-to-see-you smile. No, this was more like the sort of moronic smile you pull when you realize your rucksack has just knocked over priceless china in a gift shop.

"All right, then," I said, still looking and feeling like a right donkey. Toby stretched his arm across. The heat had melted some of the ice cream, so that little rivers of vanilla were trickling down the cone and onto Toby's fingers. For a millisecond I thought of licking up those arteries of cream, but, sensibly, I opted not to. I did pause for a brief moment, my eyes fixed on the cone, and I felt a smidgen of the charge that had gone between us just days before. Keen to avoid a sensual lick, I bit into the ice cream with my front teeth, which caused sharp pain. I played it cool and hid all signs of agony.

"Any good?" he asked.

"Mmmm. You can taste the old man's dirty fingers on it," I joked. "Wanna try my chocolate?"

"Nah, you're all right."

Toby continued smiling and staring for a bit. I returned to my ice cream, thankful he didn't want any of it, avoiding further scenes of awkward porno-shoot-esque tongue action. I felt markedly different to the way the park moment left me. I was so overcome that time, I burst into tears. This time I was slightly more in control; still very excited, confused, and charged-up, but not quite so emotional. Besides, bursting into tears in the middle of Camden Market would have been bad on several levels.

We quickly finished the ice creams off, and continued to weave our way around the hagglers, sellers, and freaks. I found an antique stall run by an Irish man with a white beard. He engaged Toby and me in light banter and wouldn't let up for around ten minutes, by which time I was considering smashing one of his precious vases just so he'd let us go. Charismatic though he undoubtedly was, the old guy really didn't need to pass the time telling us about his wife's divorce settlement and how she insisted on taking the dog if he was to keep all the antiques. Needless to say we didn't buy anything.

Toby took me to a stall he had visited several times before. He referred to the man who ran it as "Le Dude" — a fortysomething French Canadian with gapped, browning teeth and smoker's skin. He sold videos — old, new, rare — and always had a rolled-up cigarette wedged between his skew teeth. Toby was a film buff and had bought several cheap and hard-to-find tapes from Le Dude before. They greeted each other and Toby scanned the comedy section while I perused horror, coming across such exciting titles as *Mutant Aryan Kids 5* and *The Lawnmower Slaughter*. Le Dude, perched on his stool, seemed to go out of his way to be wholly unhelpful to anyone who walked in. One woman asked for *Back to the Future*, which he duly found and dumped in her general vicinity, nowhere near arm's reach. She promptly turned and left. Toby and I said our polite farewells — Le Dude grunted in our direction and rolled up another ciggy. (How he makes a living from such rudeness is beyond me.)

The Camden experience was truly eye-opening. I hadn't

witnessed diversity and weirdness on this scale before. It made me realize that Surbiton was nothing, an insignificant spot on a very large map that contained far more interesting places on it. When you're brought up in the suburbs of the South-East, you expect everywhere to be leafy, calm, and crawling with white people with sensible haircuts who talk about the weather. Camden was a revelation, and although I felt a little nervy at times, I knew I'd be back. As we returned to the Underground, I thanked Toby for showing me this melting pot. He seemed so much wiser than me, much more aware of the ways of the world. He seemed *experienced*, and I envied his confidence and his swagger. To me, it seemed like real style.

We got back on the Tube and, after being stuck in a steaming tunnel for ten minutes, arrived at Leicester Square. By now it was around 5:30, so Toby suggested we go to a cheap Chinese buffet restaurant he had tried before.

"Don't they serve chopped-up dogs in places like that?" I asked him.

"Don't be stupid," he said.

"My mum once told me she'd read about Soho Chinese restaurants having mice," I said, rather pathetically.

"Well, you don't have to order mice, you can order rat," he said.

I followed him into the "eat all you can for a tenner" joint. It was packed to the rafters, the floor space all but covered by round tables, at which sat tourist families, groups of student types, men in suits, and lots of Chinese people. Their presence reassured me and, after ordering a couple of beers, we made our way up to the enormous buffet table and stacked our plates up high.

Over this huge feast we talked some more, about nothing in particular, and then suddenly —

"So do you want a boyfriend?" Toby asked, before taking a large mouthful of sweet-and-sour. I just stared blankly at him. "Well, it's an easy question, Sam. . . ."

"No, that's just it. It's not. I don't know. I'm nowhere near ready for that kinda thing," I said.

"What kinda thing?"

"A relationship," I said with conviction. Was he making an offer, or just being an inquisitive pal?

"How about a girlfriend?"

"Maybe. Possibly. I don't know. Probably not, to be honest," I said.

We resumed our concentrated eating for a good minute, without anything being said. Toby exuded a confidence bordering on cockiness. I was beginning to resent that, and envy it at the same time. I did feel a little manipulated and taken for a ride; he knew I wasn't as single-minded or confident as he was, and he seemed to enjoy that. But, the worrying thing was, I found this terribly attractive. Over the Chinese meal I was reminded of when I first met Pod on his garden wall all those years back. Just like with Pod, I knew I was on to something. That sense of *here's someone special I know I'm going to like a lot*. With Pod, it was his zany individuality that attracted me. With Toby, it was the sureness and the swagger. I wanted a bit of it, and I guess he knew that. But with Pod, it was just a mates thing. This time there was an added dimension, and maybe it was that I fancied Toby.

It was the little things he could do that I just wouldn't. The way he got the waiter's attention with a snappy wink, the way he whipped out his debit card to pay for the bill. He seemed far more confident in the city than he did in Surbiton, and I wondered if he too felt liberated by the grandness of the location, if the sheer size of the place was enough to change his character.

After he insisted on paying for the meal, we took a wander around the backstreets of Soho, passing numerous Chinatown food stores, countless beggars, and several striptease joints. The atmosphere wasn't unlike Camden Town, but with tiny, noticeable differences. For a start, Soho was bigger, and it contained several mini-communities within it. Notably, there was an Italian bit, a Spanish bit, a CD/record shop bit, and, of course, a gay bit.

That was where Toby brought me after much meandering.

We arrived at the corner of Wardour Street and Old Compton Street. The latter is the center of the "gay village" that Toby had talked about endlessly. This street, he said, was the safest in England for gay people. Just as he made his point, a group of teens walked past, right on cue. The boy in the middle, with his short, heavily gelled hair and double-denim outfit, spoke out loudly:

"Well, beat this — I'm sixteen and I've had a nine-incher!"

You wouldn't hear *that* in the corridors of Lockham High.

We started a slow walk down Old Compton Street. Toby was all John Wayne with his strides, while I was more like Charlie Chaplin. As we moved, he became a kind of tour guide, telling me snippets about most of the establishments. There was one bar that was mainly populated by butch skinheads (male and female). Another was the scene of a bomb blast orchestrated by a Nazi nutter some years back. It was rebuilt and, in a gesture of defiance, reopened at exactly the same time at which the bomb ripped it to pieces, killing three people. We stopped outside that pub as Toby told me the story. One of those murdered was a pregnant woman. The fascist had tried to eliminate gay people, and failed horrifically.

I looked around and it really hit home just how far from Surbiton we really were. This place was like another planet. Men held hands with each other, kissing openly. I was fascinated by it all — blokes kissing in public! What the hell was going on here? And not just everyday blokes either. There were men dressed head to toe in leather, women dressed as men, men dressed as women, and people caked in so much makeup I couldn't tell what they were. Camden Town was mad enough; this place was completely off its tree. It was early evening and the road was crawling with people preparing for a night out. I wondered where they had come from. Were they night owls who spent the daytime hibernating? Were some of them businessmen who wore suspenders underneath their pinstripe suits? Were any of them from Surbiton?

It felt dirty, naughty, and yet the more I watched, the more normal it seemed, the less interesting it became.

We continued walking, passing some coffee shops with exciting pastries in the window. The choice of food outlets was almost as varied as the types of people; we decided to pause for some crepes in a cafe that looked out onto Old Compton Street. Toby ordered a bananas and cream, while I went for toffee. We sipped colas and watched the world go by. Toby looked more relaxed than I had ever seen him before.

"You have good memories of this place?" I asked, careful not to cause any upset by bringing back tortured thoughts of Paul.

"Well . . . it's funny you should say that," he began, slowly and a little hesitantly. "This all reminds me of Paul a lot," he said, and left the sentence hanging for what felt like minutes.

"Sorry, you don't have to talk about it if you don't —"

"No, no, water under the bridge, Sam. I don't mind. We came down here quite a few times, and each time I got more confident about being myself."

"You're pretty cocky today, that's for sure," I said with a smirk.

"Cocky?"

"Yeah, you just seem really . . . confident. You know."

"Yeah, I know. But it wasn't like that before. Paul has a lot to do with that. He chilled me out big time. We used to come here and he'd be all touchy-feely and trying to hold my hand and I would always keep my distance. Then one night we arranged to meet and, when I got on the train at Maidstone to come into town, I made the decision. I wouldn't be a dick anymore. This time I was gonna be myself and let Paul be himself and we were gonna have a bloody good night."

He took another bite of his bananas and cream.

"So what happened?" I asked, teeming with curiosity.

"We met, had a crepe, and snogged the life out of each other. Sitting right here, in full public view. And it felt fucking amazing. Changed me, that snog did."

Toby returned to the crepe. I suddenly felt all light-headed. Was this all part of Toby's master plan? To seduce me in a creperie over his bananas and cream? I guzzled down some cola and the caffeine rush did me good. Silence settled over us for a minute or two as we continued watching the human traffic outside. I was trying to block any thoughts of snogging Toby,

116

and so quite predictably my mind began wandering on to thoughts of Him. Where was he spending his day? Was *he* having trouble being himself? Did he fit in with that enormous group of geezers I saw him with at Waterloo? Once more, I considered telling Toby about Him, and even constructed a sentence in my head to set the ball rolling, but something stopped me from saying anything. He was to remain private.

My attention returned to the activity outside when a lunatic man began jumping up and down, shouting something about the sensationalist Sunday newspapers. Opposite, a homeless kid who couldn't have been more than sixteen was being harassed by two policemen.

As we left the creperie, Toby turned to me and put a hand on my shoulder. I swallowed hard. He looked at me with serious eyes.

"You'll be cocky too, you know," he said. "Doesn't just happen, it takes a bit of time and lots of mistakes."

I smiled and nodded. I understood exactly what he meant. And on we walked, John Wayne and Charlie Chaplin.

We hadn't gotten very far when Toby stopped.

"What is it?" I asked him.

He nodded in the direction of a bar we had stopped outside of. It was called Mission, had a blackened-out glass front, and loud house music was booming from inside. Any possibility that it wasn't a gay bar was shattered by a garish yellow poster in the middle of the black that proclaimed *Disco Fever! Wednesday nights = d-i-s-c-o at Mission, 2-4-1 drinks all night.* I looked from the poster to Toby. He was smiling cheekily. I looked very dour, and felt a panic rise within me. I had been dreading this moment from the second we stepped foot in Soho.

"What do you think? One for the road?" Toby asked.

Still I said nothing. I felt my cheeks blush as I tried to avoid eye contact with the fiend. I figured he was being genuine and probably thought that going into Mission would be a good thing for me to do.

"I'll buy you a snowball," he said, and I laughed nervously.

I went all dizzy again. The London Eye with its vast views; Camden Town with its smells, sounds and goths; a huge Chinese buffet; Soho filled with friends joined in intimacy and mutual benevolence. Too much had happened, and I was in need of a toilet for a good old-fashioned think.

I couldn't get the sensation of the sweet toffee sliding down my dry throat out of my head. I felt really, really sick, and I told Toby as much. He asked me if I wanted to pop into the bar for a glass of water. We took two paces towards Mission, but before setting foot inside, I threw up all over the pavement. Toffee crepe, pork, and noodles do not make a good combination for sick. And how is there always an orangeness in vomit even when you haven't eaten any carrots?

Toby asked me if I was all right. Sitting myself down on the curb, I assured him I was, and he didn't believe me. He scuttled into a convenience store to buy me some mineral water and a packet of tissues. Some camp passersby shouted, "Urghhh!" at me. I gave them the finger and they retaliated with a girly "Ooooh!" More surprising was the fact that most people didn't bat an eyelid. I was beginning to like this city.

However, I was still pissed off, ill, and exhausted. But most of all, I was embarrassed. A few tears forced their way out of my eye sockets and rolled on down my cheeks, pathetically. I couldn't help it. I began feeling sorry for myself. Tears have a habit of doing that. The more you cry, the more likely you are to feel shit about things. Toby returned and I wiped up my face quick. I washed my mouth out and spat the gunk into a drain. A bit like my mother would have done, Toby wiped my mouth gently with the tissues. He was being so sympathetic and selfless. For the first time since I'd met him, he'd shown me how caring he could really be.

"I'm sorry to spoil your evening," I said, one last, solitary tear dripping down my right cheek.

He told me to be quiet, and said I had done nothing of the sort. At this precise moment, he reminded me a bit of Brenda and my mum put together. He said I should drink the water until I felt better. He sat beside me and kept a hand on my back, which felt far more comforting and important than it sounds. I felt warm and safe and unlonely.

"Bet this has ruined your memories of this place," I suggested.

"No way. I'll *never* forget Old Compton Street now," he said, saying exactly the right thing at the right time, keeping his hand on my back.

I no longer felt dizzy, lightheaded, or nauseous. I leaned my head into Toby's shoulder, so that he was taking my weight and, in effect, hugging me as we sat on the pavement. My head was then resting on his chest, his left arm over my back, his hand gripping my left shoulder tight. I could feel his body's warmth, and hear his heartbeat. I looked at the people walking past, and suddenly they didn't seem quite so weird, or quite so alien, or quite so different. No one gave us a second look. The sun was slowly setting and the darkness was creeping into London. The lunatic ranted on about Sunday papers. Two policemen walked slowly. Young and old men arrived at Mission. Families left restaurants and headed for the theater. The city remained in urgent fifth gear. We didn't say a word to each other for a good ten minutes. I just sat there, in his arms, and it made sense. I didn't worry about whether this meant we were boyfriends, whether I was supposed to kiss him, whether he thought it was inappropriate. I just needed some respite, and I got it. We headed home, and although we weren't physically in each other's arms on the train, in my mind we were. I looked at him and felt lucky that I knew him so well. I looked at him and wondered if this was the start of my first relationship. And perhaps I was a step closer to being cocky. Just a step, mind.

CHAPTER 10

"IT'S HAPPY HOUR AGAIN. I THINK I MIGHT BE HAPPY IF I WASN'T OUT WITH THEM."
— THE HOUSEMARTINS

It was my third visit of the summer holiday to the Church and Abbey. Only this time, knowing that Toby was to meet me there, I was looking forward to it with some trepidation. Naturally I was skeptical as to what Pod's reaction would be to someone "gentle" like Toby, but nonetheless I knew tonight would be special. A Saturday night to remember — the night Toby entered the inner sanctum of the gang of four. Would he be approved of, grudgingly accepted, or rejected wholeheartedly? And should I care anyway? I'd found a link with Toby far stronger than anything I had with Pod or Mikey. At least Brenda was on my side, and that inspired great confidence.

I arrived by myself at around half-eight and was met by Pod, clutching six shots of tequila. He, Mikey, and Brenda were seated at a high table where I joined them. We finished off the Mexican firewater quickly, before each downing a bottle of alcopop, a garishly bright drink with, it seemed, the primary aim of coating your previously healthy white teeth with a one-inch layer of sugar.

Once the booze really started flowing, so did the offensive remarks. I'm sure these have always been made, but it was only really this summer that I noticed them, or took any offense. I'd always joined in the japes directed against minorities or weak figures. I'd even partaken of some verbal bullying at school, taking the piss out of anyone remotely different from anyone else. So maybe I was getting what I deserved, but Mikey was meant to be a mate.

"I mean let's face it, guys . . . there are two types of people in this world: poofs, and people who are all right."

He and Pod laughed hysterically as Brenda did her best to calm them. But Mikey wouldn't let it lie. Ever the clown, he decided to have a go at me for the way I drank my bottle of alcopop.

"Oh, Sam! Would you not drink your bottle like that, please?" He pulled a sour face.

"Like what?" I asked, genuinely lost.

"All seductively."

"You're bloody paranoid, mate."

Pod piped up: "No, Sam's used to something softer."

This was just getting silly now. But for Pod, the floodgates had opened, and, fueled by alcohol, he asked me the sorts of personal questions he was too embarrassed to ask when sober:

"Talking of softer, how's Toby? Mikey said he saw you two having a hug. What would the Rangers think about that, eh?"

White Jeans had obviously been gossiping with Pod behind my back. I was reminded of a small but nasty remark Mikey made to Toby as training ended: "Sure you got the bollocks for this?" Toby didn't grace the insult with a reply, but this continuous barrage provoked me.

"You were bloody rude to him the other night, Mikey. He was only trying to be friendly."

"That was the problem," said Pod. Very funny.

"Leave him alone, will you?" I said.

Mikey spotted space for a cheap gag. "Oooh . . . touchy, are we?"

Pod filled the space accordingly. "Well, he is with Toby, too right!"

I walked into it when I said, "I'm not going to rise to it."

"You don't have to, mate — Toby's already risen," said Mikey, himself a frequent "riser" during school lessons. For Brenda, all this mickey-taking was going too far. She made a stand, and told Pod they were leaving.

"I'm not going anywhere, I've only had two," said Pod, blatantly lying.

"Well, you can piss off, then, you offensive twat," spat Brenda. For a girl to call her partner of three years a twat and mean it, the offense has to be pretty offensive. But I guess Brenda was a true mate of mine, and true mates don't like to see each other get hurt. Particularly not by other, supposedly true mates. She began to gather her things. Pod was clearly upset.

"What about . . . y'know. . . ?" he whispered in Brenda's general direction.

"You can forget about *that*. Not that it really matters, 'coz you'll only get brewer's droop, like most nights. Or if it's not brewer's droop it's beer breath and curry vomit in the morning."

Mikey greeted the brewer's droop remark with a huge laugh.

123

The rest of us just stared at him. He stopped laughing pretty sharpish. This was no joking matter; it was far worse than the "offensive twat." She had hit Pod where it hurt. Although ninety percent of the time he looked like a nasty piece of work, Pod wasn't hugely built, and his face still told the truth. And at this moment it melted. I felt sorry for him, and given that he'd just been an offensive twat, that was quite something.

"That's out of order, Brenda," said Pod, apologetically.

"Well, so are you. Why can't you leave Sam alone? Since we've got back it's been piss-take after piss-take."

Mikey stepped in, apparently as some sort of peacemaking mediator.

"Chill out, Brenda, we're just having a laugh. Anyway, it's Toby we're dissing, not Sam. You don't mind, do you, Sam, mate?"

I looked him in the eye. "No, I don't mind, mate." No sarcasm, of course.

Mikey, having apparently diffused the situation and saved Brenda and Pod's relationship, looked annoyingly smug.

"There. Relax, Brenda. Let's not spoil the evening now," he said.

Brenda wanted some closure, which in her book meant having the last word in this dispute. She stared at Pod accusingly.

"You might be my boyfriend, but he's still my best friend, got it?"

"I'm sorry, Brends," he said.

I decided it was time *I* stepped in as peacekeeper. I'd kept quiet, probably because I did feel rather hard done-by, and wanted Pod to receive some sort of punishment.

"Brenda, really, it's OK. If you can't laugh at yourself —"

"Exactly . . . Sam doesn't mind a bit of piss-taking," interrupted Mikey. Well, I *did* mind, but I was in no mood for a big row, especially not with the amount of booze we'd all drunk.

"You see," said Pod, "not all batty boys are twats."

Mikey spat his beer out as he laughed. For Pod, it was a drunken social experiment — how far could he push his girlfriend? And if she was really in love with him, would she forgive his laddish nastiness? Or would she side with the sensitive best friend? For Brenda, it was the excuse she needed to properly register her disgust, not only at their treatment of me, but, I suspected, at Pod's changing ways. He'd always been Jack-the-lad, but since his year at university, he'd come back a lot more aggressive. At school, he always made the odd homophobic joke, or remark about spastic people, but he returned from Leeds with a new streak of malicious nastiness. His homophobic comments trebled, probably because he was so worried about the implications of a best friend being . . . unstraight. Pod seemed a whole lot more defensive, angry, and like something out of the Stone Age. Not a pretty sight. Brenda grabbed her bag and, without a word, left.

"I think you took it a bit far, mate," suggested Mikey.

"She's oversensitive. She'll be all right," Pod concluded as he finished off his pint, making no attempt to go after his girlfriend. "Your round, White Jeans."

Mikey went to get the drinks, screaming, "Bird of prey," and groping the air with his hands as though he was feeling a pair of boobs. The more Mikey did things like that, the more I thought he was still a virgin.

Pod and I were left alone on our barstools, the packed pub around us, with its guffawing, happy punters distant and unhelpful to us in our uneasy silence. We hadn't been alone together since coming back from uni.

"Right, why is it, yeah, that women are allowed to talk about blokes they fancy, but if a bloke even mentions another girl he gets a slap? And right, why is it they don't like you having female friends? I mean, where's the trust? Bloody unfair if you ask me."

I figured that Pod was trying to tell me something. Brenda, I guessed, had frowned upon some of Pod's female friends at Leeds, or perhaps she was upset that he'd described a girl as "fit." Either way, this was Pod's attempt at breaking the deadlock, at reaching out and being mates. Although I suspected he was trying to stave off any criticism from me about his treatment of Brenda moments earlier, he still seemed to be talking from the heart. Having never had a proper relationship with a girl, I offered my best, inexperienced analysis for some comfort.

"They want to control us," I said tentatively. "I can't blame them, really. We're bloody useless at the best of times."

I was pleased with this — two gender stereotypes in one, and a bit of self-deprecation while I was at it. Pod, however, looked lost. He either didn't get what I had just said or didn't want to get it. So as was always the case when conversation dried up, or when Pod felt stupid, he turned the attention to tits and lipstick.

"Quite a bit of talent tonight."

"What about Brenda?" I asked, half jokingly.

"No, I meant for you. . . . You know I'm a hundred percent faithful."

I scanned the pub full of youngsters. "Well, you're right, there is a bit of talent."

Pod looked down at his empty pint glass. "So . . . you and Toby . . . you guys are just mates, right?"

He'd pissed me off again. "I don't fancy him, Pod. I'm not queer." Admittedly this wasn't the whole truth, but I figured Pod wouldn't really understand my complicated definition issues, and it seemed the easiest way of getting him off my back.

"Yeah, course, I knew that. I am still your mate, you know."

Pod had a knack of saying the wrong thing at the wrong time, as demonstrated earlier in the evening. I retaliated with a —

"Oh, I get it, so if I *was* queer, you wouldn't be my mate?"

I left this conveniently as half-statement, half-question. Pod looked exasperated, and started inadvertently spitting a lot when he spoke.

"No, that's not it. Do you get off on feeling hated or something? I only wanted to help you pull."

"Well, thanks for the offer, but no thanks," I said.

"Not pull me, you moron!" he shouted, not realizing how he was showing himself up as the moron. I just rolled my eyes as Mikey returned with the drinks. He looked a bit miffed.

"What does *belligerent* mean?" he asked.

"It means *sexy*. It's a posh way of saying *fit*," I said.

Mikey's miff turned to delight at the merest hint of potential action.

"Yeah? Fuck you, lads. Finish my beer and I'm in!"

As he said this, I spotted Toby. He was looking good, as per usual, in a polo shirt, dark blue jeans, and skater trainers. He found our table, we said our hellos, and he gave me a quick hug. My eyes quickly looked about the pub.

"Oh, for fuck's sake . . . do you have to?" Pod said. Throughout the whole of the subsequent exchange, he avoided eye contact with Toby.

"Pod, Toby, Toby, Pod," I nervously said, getting the introductions out of the way.

"So nice to meet you too," Toby said sarcastically.

"I have views," announced Pod, like some sort of politician. "And there's no need to be so public. You don't see me and Brenda all over each other in the pub."

Mikey pitched in:

"Don't see you and Brenda over each other at all, mate."

Pod ignored him. His verbal assault was well into its stride. "People are staring. They never used to, and I don't like that."

I defended Toby's presence. He was my friend, and if I wanted him to come out with us, then he would. "I see. You're pissed off 'coz you think someone'll start a ruck, right?"

"He attracts attention and I don't wanna get into a fight," was Pod's rather feeble response. By now, Toby had planned his ripostes to perfection and was ready to go in for the verbal kill.

"Why are you so repressed? Why do you get so uncomfortable and jealous?" he asked, sounding a bit like an American chat-show host. "If everybody else is cool with it, why aren't you?"

"White Jeans isn't cool with it — you get the hump, don't you?"

Mikey unwittingly destroyed Pod's case. "Well, I take the mick but I don't really give a shit, mate."

Toby kept on with the questions. "Why do you have to call us fruits?"

"Because you're a shirtlifter."

"Would you sort your life out?" Quite a deep question, that

one. A little unfair, I thought. Then a question that was brilliantly simple.

"Right, why are you called Pod?"

"'Coz I am, I always have been since I can remember."

"And I've liked boys and girls since I can remember. It's just me. Like you're just Pod, it's what I am."

This was the first time Toby had said, in a clear and unapologetic way, that he was attracted to both genders. It took us all by surprise; I think Mikey and Pod had never knowingly experienced a nonstraight firsthand before. Eventually, Pod composed himself, and brought the argument back to his beloved name.

"But my name's natural."

"Natural? There's nothing natural about the name Pod!" Toby had a point here.

"Better than being a poof," was the best Pod could come up with now. "Besides . . . just 'coz you've always liked boys and girls, doesn't mean you've got to try and convert Sam."

I couldn't believe the bullshit Pod was spouting. Toby just smirked and said, "You really are a mess. I'm growing to feel sorry for you, mate."

He put a hand on Pod's shoulder, and Pod made eye contact for the first time. He grabbed Toby's hand and stood up.

"Get off me! I don't like people staring and I don't wanna get into a fight, but I will if I have to."

Toby continued smirking. I was in total awe of him. He didn't seem particularly angry or bitter, probably because he knew he was in the right. He genuinely felt sorry for Pod and his ignorance.

Mikey interrupted the tension with a rendition of "one

129

Church and Abbey, there's only one Church and Abbey," his usual pub chant.

Moments later, Pod recognized someone from school and went over to chat. Mikey left to chat up the girl who had called him belligerent. Surprisingly, he ended up snogging her. As I sat on my bathroom toilet that night, I wondered why pretty and seemingly pleasant girls end up kissing sexist loudmouths. What is it about that blatant pulling technique that works? And why doesn't being a nice bloke ever seem to work with girls? Mikey's departure had the pluspoint of leaving Toby and me alone. By now, with a little time to reflect, I was getting upset at Pod's comments and deep-rooted hatred. Toby kept telling me not to worry about it, that Pod was the one who had the problems. But as I kept telling Toby, the whole thing was made a lot more painful by the fact I didn't really know whether Pod was right or not. Was I like Toby — did I fancy boys and girls? — or did I just like boys a lot as friends, or did I feel closer to them than girls, and does sex define sexuality, and if I wanted to hug and hold hands but nothing more, did that make me gay or bi? My state of mind was as tangled as a bowl of spaghetti. And just when I was thrashing out these major issues with Toby, and him telling me not to worry, which had the reverse effect, The Most Beautiful Girl in the World™ walked in.

We were both standing at the bar when this five-foot-nine, leggy beauty approached. She had long, light brown hair, perfect skin, aqua-blue eyes, and cute freckles. She stood right next to me, and I noticed Toby staring at her. I copied.

"Do I have 'ignore me' written on my forehead?" she asked nobody in particular.

"Pardon?" I said, in a bit of a daze.

"Has somebody graffitied 'ignore me' on my forehead?" she said, this time turning to face me. I realized she was referring to the bar staff's delay in serving her.

"Oh no," I said, "I think the staff here have very short memories, that's all."

Lame, but an icebreaker at least.

Then, just when things were going so smoothly, Toby had to join in with a "hiya." The girl's response was unexpected.

"Not a local, are you?"

"I study in town. Why d'you ask?" replied Toby.

"Locals don't say 'hiya' to girls at the bar. Conversations normally start with 'all right, love, fancy a shag?'"

"Sam's a local. . . ."

Toby laughed, and I felt tiny. That was low — a friend making the other look stupid to impress a girl. I might have expected it from Mikey — in fact, I'd grown used to it — but from Toby? It sucked. I tried to regain some composure and input into the conversation.

"Thank you, Toby. But you're a local too, right?" I asked her.

"Not for long." Shite. Everything I said seemed wrong. "I've passed my A Levels," she said. "I'm going to university. Liverpool."

I offered her some congratulations and we all swapped names. Hers was Lucy. Lovely feminine name. Quite sweet, I always thought. Better than Sam Smith, of course. Toby made another suggestion —

"Look, I tell you what, why don't we buy your drink and bring it over. Where are you sitting?"

"Are you sure?" asked Lucy, in the way that people do when they know full well you're going to say, "Of course, no problem."

"Course. No problem," said Toby.

"That's really kind," she said, and I began to feel mildly nauseous. But I played along, because I thought she was fit. And no, it had nothing to do with the fact Toby and her were hitting it off so well.

"But I'll get the next round, OK?" said Lucy.

"No problem," said Toby.

"Are you sure?" Yes!

"Absolutely," is what I actually said.

"All right. See you in a minute, then."

"Absolutely," said Toby, although I wasn't sure if it was a deliberate imitation of me. This was a very weird moment. I'd met Toby, got totally confused about my feelings for him, and suddenly here we were in my local pub following a huge bust-up with Pod looking lustily at the same girl. A few moments of silence followed Lucy's departure. I broke it.

"What d'you think?" I asked.

"Special. Rare sort for these parts."

"Could get well wrapped in a girl like that."

"Don't know about you, mate, but she's flicked my switch."

Until this point, we were just spouting compliments about her, oblivious to the other's comments. But the "flicked my switch" remark flicked a switch in my head; I realized now that he meant it.

"You fancy her, then?" I asked.

"Who wouldn't?" he asked back.

"You want her, then?"

"Course I do."

"You'll chase her, then?"

"Yes!"

A pause while I thought of something useful to say.

"I saw her first."

"Bollocks!"

"No no, fair's fair."

"I saw her too."

"Yeah, but you can't chase her."

"I want her, I'm going to give it a go, and I'm going to get her," he said, and I had no reason to doubt his determination. A war had been declared, and I wasn't going to stand back and be bombarded with personal attacks.

"You'll do nothing of the sort," I said defiantly. Jesus, I must have sounded like some chivalric hero defending the dame from a nasty adulterer.

"Noth — nothing of the sort? Who's stopping me?"

"Me. I saw her first. I lay claim to her by seeing her first. If you wanna stab me in the back, go ahead but that's it, you can find yourself a new best friend."

A little melodramatic, granted, but I was desperate here.

"I don't believe this. This is nuts. I'm going to chat her up, Sam, and you can't stop me. If you can't take that, that's your problem, not mine."

"You're my friend!" I reminded him.

"Well, obviously you don't think I'm good enough for her."

"No, but I think you're out of line if you chase her. Loyalty, Toby, loyalty."

"You're mad. Childish and mad."

And he was off to get her, leaving me to buy the drinks, of course. I shouted, "Don't!" after him but he ignored me. I'll admit my argument was a tad unreasonable, but I *had* seen her first. Needless to say Toby pulled her, much to my disapproval.

While they were kissing, I thought, *Sod it,* and kissed Lucy's mate, Emma. She had shoulder-length brown hair, summer-tanned skin, and big tits. She made good small talk, and seemed very polite and all that, but she wasn't really my thing. Emma was to kissing what Adolf Hitler was to tolerance.

When I got home that night, I took some time out on the loo. I figured that I'd only kissed Emma because Toby had stabbed me in the back. Bloody shameful. He could have done so much better for himself. But I guess it's hard when someone you like makes mistakes. I wondered if Toby actually liked me, like Brenda had speculated, but didn't know it, or denied it. I knew and know too well how easy it can be to bury your true feelings so deep you don't even know you have them. Maybe that's why he pulled Lucy — because he actually wanted to pull me. Whatever his motivation, I felt really lonely that night. I sat on the shitter and felt less important, like I'd been snubbed. I realized just how much I liked him as a person, not his looks or his clothes — him. And that night, I felt like I'd lost a bit of him, like he'd given himself over to somebody else. And I missed him.

CHAPTER 11

THE CUCKOO WRASSE AND THE COUPLE

There is a cabinet at the London Aquarium that displays items recovered from the depths of the River Thames. It contains objects as diverse as a portable television set, a plastic toy, £140 cash, and a coconut on a plate. There's also a cattle bone, a casino chip, an alarm clock, and a jar of chili peppers in vinegar.

Most interesting of all are the objects that, in my mind, have a story behind them. I had found myself being very inquisitive, not just about my own life, but about everybody else's. So it seemed only right to ask myself: How did these things end up in the river? Why were they thrown? Who threw them?

I stood there, beside the cabinet, considering how the numerous mobile phones had found their way to the riverbed. A telephone argument between lovers resulting in a furious mid-conversation hurl into the water below? Perhaps a worker being told he or she was fired? Was it a last-resort reaction to a text stalker? Or was it plain fury at the telephone's poor signal?

Why were so many phones being thrown in the river? Carelessness, or acts of anger and attempts to start anew?

I wondered about the date stamp, fixed on 27 August 1979. Was it a hot August? Was it a pissed-off secretary? Where did she work? What did secretaries do to while away the hours before the Internet?

It's times like this when I really feel different from my mates.

I visited the London Aquarium on my second London excursion with Toby, precisely a week after the pub fiasco. We had one dull training session in that time, during which Pretty Boy Pete kept hobbling off the pitch in pain, and Mikey was strangely quiet. Meanwhile, off the field, Pod had all but disappeared, and Brenda wasn't talking to him.

Toby text-messaged me to suggest another trip into town, and despite the barfing incident on Old Compton Street, I figured I was probably a lot more confident about things than I was the first time we went up. Maybe this could be an opportunity, away from prying eyes again, to work out what we meant to each other, and to patch things up.

It wasn't until we met at Surbiton train station that I realized Lucy would be coming, too.

No working out what we meant to each other, then.

Abso-bloody-lutely wonder-fucking-ful.

Any illusion that this might be Toby's attempt to seduce me in a Soho bar went right out the window with her arrival, arm in arm with him. And to make matters worse, she was looking her usual, effortlessly stunning self in a summery white top and cool, tight jeans.

"You don't mind if Lucy comes with, do you, Sam?"

"Course not. Hi, Lucy," I said flatly.

If she took offense at my unenthusiastic response, she didn't show it. She kissed me on the cheek and squeezed my arm, which I found a little strange given that I hardly knew her at all. A kiss is one thing, an arm squeeze is quite another.

We boarded the delayed, filthy train and headed for London. The twenty-minute journey was hot, sweaty, and not very comfortable. Toby and Lucy held hands throughout, and occasionally looked into each other's eyes longingly and annoyingly and kissed on the lips. We made polite conversation about the weather, Pod, beer prices, and so forth. Then they told me about their first date, which had taken place a few days previously; a cringe-worthy Wednesday evening spent watching the same dire romantic comedy Pod, Brenda, and I had been subjected to at the local multiplex. Toby and Lucy both raved about it, which baffled me, but I did the polite thing and smiled, saying, "It was definitely romantic" — shockingly perceptive of me. After the dross, Toby had taken Lucy to an Italian restaurant on the High Street. She described it as "swanky," but I've been there with my mum and, frankly, it's nothing more than mediocre. As Toby prattled on about what he had to eat, I was reminded of the restaurant's painful resident band — a husband-and-wife team who play middle-of-the-road hits on a crappy keyboard and electric guitar. The sort of music only a hen- or stag-night group would dance to. It was at this point Lucy told me that Toby had asked her up to dance. I looked disbelievingly at him, but he avoided eye contact. Maybe he realized his girlfriend was inadvertently making me feel awkward. After all, Lucy had no idea what was going on between me and Toby. And I would have probably been upset, were it not for the comic value of imagining Toby and Lucy dancing to that pair of middle-aged never-weres.

I didn't know where to look when, minutes later, they started playing touchy-feely happy couple, and my fidgety fingers must have given away how awkward I felt. I didn't think they were putting on a show to make me feel shitty, but they may as well have done, complete with an opening song, jazz hands, and pyrotechnic effects in the background on each kiss (the sparks as the wheels ran across the train tracks provided that anyway). Brenda and Pod had never made me feel so left out.

The happy couple was being appallingly happy, and I was asking myself why on earth they had invited me along. I was convinced Toby and I were going to continue where we had left off in Old Compton Street. I had even spent the previous night tossing and turning in my bed as I considered all the possible outcomes and events of the day. I pondered how I would say hello to Toby when we met, what type of food we would eat, whether or not I'd let him pay, and how we would end the evening (I was still rather nervous about the Soho gay scene, but ready to give it a try).

None of this was to be.

Lucy suggested we check out the aquarium, which she had heard good things about. I must confess I was interested in seeing the fish too, especially the sharks. Toby wasn't going to disagree with both of us, although I sensed he would have preferred another attraction. It was the first time since I was a little kid that I had gone to London with the express intention of doing a tourist thing, and I was quite excited. Besides, I thought it would give me a good opportunity to look at something other than Toby and Lucy for a couple of hours.

The aquarium is a short walk from London Waterloo station, so we marched over in the baking midday sun and carved our way through hordes of tourists and school groups along the South Bank. Some French children were showing off the English swear words they had learned to each other, which made Lucy laugh.

The London Eye, meanwhile, stood above us, watching over the city.

"God, that was great fun up there, wasn't it, Toby?" I asked. Lucy looked at me.

"Yeah, I enjoyed the Eye," said Toby.

Lucy seemed a little put out. Surely she wasn't jealous that Toby and I had done something sociable that she hadn't been involved in?

After paying at the reception desk, we entered the underground sea world that is the London Aquarium. A long, dark corridor filled with the sound FX of splashing waves greeted us. Toby and Lucy held hands. Their persistent intimacy was a little weird — after all, this was only their second date. I wondered if they had slept together, but this thought gave me an empty gut. I still couldn't quite understand why I was there.

The aquarium was something special. You can't help but watch the charismatic fish, sometimes losing yourself inside the tank for minutes on end (not literally, although that could be fun too). The aquarium is to fish what Camden and Soho is to people. Koi carp, sticklebacks, sting rays, pilotfish, starfish, the lethal lionfish, bass, bream, jellyfish . . . the list went on. They all looked so different. Perhaps my senses weren't attacked in quite the way they were when Toby and I exited Camden Town tube a week or so before, but nonetheless there was a similar sense of variety and excitement, without any of the fear.

We were all very interested in the tanks and the various information boards. I did notice, however, that whenever I called Toby over and showed him something, Lucy would become a little impatient and start blowing in his ear, or stroking his back. On a couple of occasions, by the venomous stonefish, I deliberately grabbed his attention just as she was trying to feel him. I don't think she noticed my tactic. It seems a little childish to me now, but the aquarium was hardly the place to be physically intimate.

After perusing the rivers and ponds zone and the huge Atlantic tank, we walked up to the even huger Pacific to witness the thrice-weekly shark feed. This was an event and a half. There are no human-eating sharks at the aquarium, but the sand tiger, brown, nurse, and zebra sharks look pretty vicious and you wouldn't want to spend time in a Jacuzzi with them. We stood with several other spectators, many of them noisy kids, watching in awe as the bits of dead fish that make up dinner were chucked into the water. The tranquil ambient music playing all around was at odds with the display of savage dining in front of us. The soundtrack really was calming, though; one woman had managed to fall asleep sitting by the tank glass and missed the entire feed.

The non-shark members of the Pacific sea life (sting rays, pilotfish, jacks) were forced to wait around patiently for bits of fish rejected by their shark superiors. I noticed a fish head float to the bottom of the tank, unwanted. It remained there, untouched, its open eyes looking ghoulishly at me.

I turned from the fascinating animal behavior to see another form of it going on right behind me. Toby and Lucy were engaged in a full-scale snog.

"You're missing the feed," I said.

Toby seemed a little embarrassed.

"Sorry, mate. What's happening?" he asked me, trying to sound genuine. Lucy just smiled.

Annoyed at being called "mate," I turned back towards the Pacific tank, and winked at Florence, the nurse shark.

We moved on around the exhibition and I must say that Lucy's marine knowledge was very impressive. She obviously had a keen interest in the subject, due in no small part to her father's keen hobby of fishing, which she often assisted him with. She was also clued up on the environmental issues. We went to the seashore zone where you can touch several creatures native to the British coast. I thought Toby was taking the piss when he took Lucy's hand and, together, they dipped into the water and touched a starfish. I stood next to them feeling like a right lemon. This scene was like a bad 80s pop video. All the happy couple needed were rolled-up jackets, ankle warmers, and big, blow-dried hair. After a short while of watching their hideously corny fish-fondling, I decided to give one of the crabs a feel. But I struck the water with such ferocity that the splash went all over a girl beside me.

Toby and Lucy were, for a lot of the time in the aquarium, behaving as though I wasn't there. There were other couples everywhere and I felt a little out of place. I found empathy by the poison frog tank, where I noticed a young Mediterranean boy of about four who was trying to communicate with an English boy of the same age, unaware that they spoke different languages.

I was feeling so uncomfortable that I even considered excusing myself and leaving the happy couple to it, but on a few occasions Lucy tore herself away from Toby and, linking arms with me, walked about the place comparing notes on favorite fish. I was particularly keen on the sturgeon with its long, beaky nose, while Lucy preferred the flashlight fish, which has a freaky light glowing from its head. The three of us stared at the darkened flashlight tank for a while, transfixed by the fish's bright glow. The chilled-out mood music was everywhere, although I couldn't find the speakers that played it. I watched the bubbles rise hypnotically in the water and, looking through the tank glass, noticed how the passersby became stretched and twisted.

Toby went to the toilet just as we reached the pufferfish display. These are the most poisonous fish in the world, their bright, mazelike bodies giving us the hint that they won't make good sushi. Unfortunately, none are kept at the aquarium. Lucy and I read the display board.

"Pretty scary, huh?" I said, feeling immediately silly.

"I suppose they're only trying to survive."

"Maybe I should wear a very bright tracksuit with a maze on it."

She chuckled. "I don't think it'd flatter you, Sam," she said.

We continued with this fluff for a short while, until Toby returned. They held hands.

I stared at a tank in the coral reef section, sitting myself down on the sill by the glass. The happy couple sauntered around the other tanks behind me. I remember thinking how the weird fish faces reminded me of human ones. Some looked like stuffy shopkeepers, others like bored accountants, and a few like gray lecturers, while the odd one or two resembled exotic women, and one reminded me of a slimmer Harry. Even some of the crabs and poison frogs rang bells in my head. I read that over a hundred different fish, invertebrates, and totally new species were discovered each year in our waters. That made me feel insignificant. For a few seconds, at least. But not as insignificant as Toby was making me feel.

I was convinced the fish weren't just opening and closing their mouths like gormless idiots. No way, José. They were singing and protesting. It couldn't be pleasant going from a nice big ocean to a small tank in central London. I was positive they were singing to remain cheerful (and mouth off about the state they were in). Then they forgot about it all, what with the six-second memory and that, and started all over again, cursing their luck.

I was also convinced that the cuckoo wrasse fish were talking to themselves. Their mouth movements weren't the usual, big goldfish-like ones. They were definitely muttering something. I saw one of these cuckoo wrasse vomit and then swim away and hide behind a rock. I was growing to really like these fish. I almost forgot about Lucy and Toby as I gazed into the tanks. Oh, to be a fish. I was engrossed in their world. How did they feel, if they felt at all? In my uncomfortable state, I even found myself wondering if a rock hermit crab might feel like a third wheel too, if another couple of rock hermits were getting it on close by.

Lucy was particularly taken with the large tank full of piranha fish. She explained to me that they're not as deadly as you think, and only attack if provoked. She said one of her ambitions was to visit the Amazon and go swimming with piranhas.

"You're mad!" I said, feeling relaxed around her for the first time.

She laughed. "That's what my dad says."

I couldn't help but feel the piranhas had done their bit to bring Lucy and me a little closer, but her interaction with Toby still made for uneasy viewing. We continued to walk. They held hands.

We came to a display on pipefish and sea horses. I was amazed to read about how they breed; the crafty female lays the eggs in a pouch on the male's underside and he is the one who gives birth. As I reread the display, and wondered what would happen if women dumped the fetus with the bloke and forced him to give birth — certain infant mortality, I concluded — Toby tapped me on the shoulder.

"You really like this place, don't you?" he asked me, all smiles.

"Yeah, it's great. Seriously, those coral reef fish remind me of the Rangers. They've all got these funny faces. It's brilliant." I was overdoing it on the cheeriness to conceal my anger. I immediately wished I'd been more up-front.

Once we'd seen all there was to see, checking out some tanks twice or even three times, we went into the gift shop. I considered buying one of the *Tranquil Waves* CDs that had made the shark-feeding experience so surreal, but decided against it. I did, however, buy an overpriced photo book on marine life, which I've looked at almost daily ever since.

Then a weird thing happened.

I turned from the till, put my wallet back in my pocket, and noticed a stand of name cards. These are big sellers in gift shops, cards that explain the traditional characteristics of people with certain names. So, for example, for Joanne it might say, "A courageous person, inclined to follow not lead, and very loyal, but occasionally lazy." Something like that.

The revolving rack on which these cards were kept was quite big, and I looked intently at it, searching out one name in particular. Someone was beside me, half turned towards me. I didn't pay much attention to whoever it was. Then suddenly both our hands reached for the same name card. We looked up at each other and laughed apologetically, then our eyes widened a little in surprise. The other person was Lucy. We were both stretching for the Toby name card.

"You first," she said.

"OK," I said, then read from the card. " 'Toby, short masculine and feminine form of the Biblical Tobias.' " Well, this was a shocker for a start. I thought Toby was quite a male name, but this definition made a lot of sense. I continued, " 'Tobias is a heroic figure in the Old Testament. The name means *God is good*. A Toby is calm, measured, and of great intentions. Whilst he will please many, he may disappoint others. He is confident, opinionated, and honest.' "

Lucy and I looked at each other questioningly.

"And is it true?" she asked. She acknowledged for the first time that I knew Toby better than she did, and I appreciated that.

"Kind of, I guess. I don't believe in these things too much," I said, replacing the card.

"No, neither do I. Probably written by an old bloke in a shed somewhere."

I smiled, and Toby joined us.

"Name cards. These things are a load of old bollocks, aren't they?"

"We were just saying that," I said, conscious of using "we" for the first time in relation to Lucy and me.

Looking back now from the safety of the toilet, I can honestly say that, although their behavior annoyed the hell out of me, I didn't really blame Lucy. Toby was the guilty party. He knew the score with me and she didn't. OK, so maybe she could have been a little less hands-on, but she had no idea about all the shit going through my head at that time. She was all right really, and my God did she look great in that top. She fitted in nicely in the coral reef zone, reminding me of a swimwear model.

As we all walked out of the bookshop, Lucy promised to take me and Toby fishing one day. I gave her an enthusiastic response. She asked me about Emma.

"You called her yet? I think she likes you."

I began avoiding Lucy's eyes.

"Nah, she's not really my type. Besides, I'm not on the lookout for a . . . relationship right now, to be honest," I said.

"Well, one date wouldn't hurt," she suggested.

"Yeah, why not give her a try, mate?" said Toby.

"Look, I'm not interested in Emma," I snapped.

I didn't like him calling me the "m" word. It was the word Pod and Mikey used, and Toby meant more than that to me. It was a term that was meant to be affectionate, but that was actually cold and meaningless. He'd used it more that day than he ever had before, and I couldn't help thinking that he wanted

Lucy to think we were ordinary, run-of-the-mill friends. Maybe, in his mind, that *was* all we were.

We went to a pizza parlor nearby for some quatro formaggi. I sat on one side of the table; they sat opposite, occasionally feeding bits of food into each other's mouths. I made no attempt at hiding my disapproval.

Toby definitely noticed the *fuck off* vibes on my face, and he let up a little bit.

Lucy, meanwhile, wanted to know more about us.

"How long you been friends, then? Seems like you know each other quite well," she said.

"Could say that, yeah," was all I offered by way of a reply.

"We've actually only been friends for a few weeks," said Toby.

"Is that all? Feels like so much longer, what with everything that's happened," I said. "Or have you forgotten already?"

"No," he said sharply.

"Good. Thought you had."

"Look, Sam, if you're —"

"If I'm what?"

"What's the matter?"

"Nothing's the matter, what could possibly be the matter?"

Lucy looked at me, then at Toby, and sensed the simmering prickles. She expertly changed the subject to her hopes for the future, when she left for Liverpool University. She talked of maybe becoming a vet in a few years' time. I couldn't help but find this all a bit funny, her talking about a new phase of her life that would almost certainly spell the end of her new relationship with Toby.

"How do you find living at home, Sam?" she asked.

"It's OK. I get on pretty well with my mum. She does her thing and lets me do mine."

"That's lucky. My mum and me are always arguing. Liverpool's just about far away enough for me," she said, smiling.

The conversation continued at a very stunted pace. None of us looked very comfortable, and I certainly didn't feel at ease. It was Toby's fault for being so bloody insensitive. He was like one of those color-changing cuttlefish we had seen. He remained the same person, but kept changing, with noticeable character differences. Was it too much to ask him not to flirt incessantly with his new girl right in front of me?

I refused to accept he was deliberately trying to wind me up by being so lovey-dovey with Lucy. It had to be ignorance on his part, but then this was Mr. Experienced Confident Cocky I've Had a Boyfriend. He was supposed to understand. Instead, he left me feeling about as big as a minnow. Sure, he was polite and charming as ever, but the warmth and closeness that he had shown me before — especially during our last London visit — vanished. His true fondness was reserved for Lucy.

I became a little emotional at the dinner table, and couldn't stomach another bite of the cheesy pizza. The happy couple had calmed down a bit on the touching, and I noticed Lucy occasionally move Toby's hand away. She seemed to be understanding me a little better.

I excused myself and went to the toilet, where I found a comfortable and clean seat to perch on, lid down, trousers up.

I blew my nose on the bristly toilet paper and instantly regretted it.

A thousand and one things went through my mind. The day's events, of course, interspersed with recurring images of that bloody flashlight fish and its glowing lantern head. Lucy's favorite fish was haunting me. I tugged at my hair and slapped myself around the face.

One thing was for sure: The three of us weren't compatible. I couldn't hack another occasion alone with them. I wasn't sure if I could tolerate seeing them together at all. Every time they touched, it sent me into frustration overdrive. I stayed on the toilet seat in that restaurant for a good ten minutes. Nobody knew about my shitter shenanigans — so when I got back to the table after my lengthy absence, Toby asked, "You all right, mate?"

"Yes . . . mate. I'm fine," I replied, slowly and pointedly.

The train journey back to Surbiton was painful. For the most part, we sat in embarrassed silence, for which I felt partly guilty. They held hands.

Then, after almost twenty minutes of staring out of windows and laughing at a small girl who kept on stabbing her mother with a plastic sword, Toby piped up.

"You know Bliss, Sam . . ." he said, knowing full well I knew about Surbiton's gay club.

"Yeah, I told Brenda about it. Why?"

"How about it?"

I wasn't sure if he meant just the two of us, or if he was considering a big night with Lucy there too. But, with Brenda having said she would accompany me, I was prepared to give it a go. I felt confident there would be no nervous nausea this time.

"Why not?" I said.

The train pulled into the station, and we got off, making our way to the station forecourt.

"I'll text you," Toby said.

"OK, cool," I said.

"Thanks for a great day," Lucy said.

"OK, cool," I said.

I was expecting her to leave, and for Toby and me to walk home, maybe going the long way through the park as we had done before. The least he could have given me was a walk home, after a day of making me feel like a total mong.

"See you, then," he said.

"OK, cool," I said.

They turned, holding hands, and walked away.

I stood in the forecourt, the black cabs roaring around me.

That empty feeling was rising through my abdomen. Toby had hurt me, yet I couldn't help but realize — the reason it hurt so much was because I liked the guy.

I really, really liked the guy.

CHAPTER 12

COMBAT FLOUR

Having not heard from Brenda for a week, and concerned at her lack of a reply to any of my text messages, I called her up when I got home from the aquarium. I was feeling pretty shitty, but she sounded a lot worse. Pod had really upset her this time, and I couldn't recall ever hearing her in such a state. I offered to come over, but she said she'd rather chat on the phone. And chat we did, for almost two hours.

Combining Brenda's detailed and rather upset account of the evening with my own imagination, I sat on the toilet at home and went through the events of the pub fiasco night, a little shocked and — dare I say it? — flattered that I had managed to cause such a ruckus.

Brenda's parents were out for the night, and her kid brother was staying over at his aunt's house, so Brenda was all alone. She had returned from her huff at the pub, turned on the TV, and opened a jumbo size packet of crisps to calm her nerves. After about an hour, at just past eleven o'clock, the doorbell rang. She knew who it would be, and considered not answering it. But then Pod, with more than a few drinks inside him, opened the letterbox and began shouting.

"Brends, it's me. Go on, let me in. I won't get narky, Brenda. Please, we need to talk about things."

Brenda shouted back from the living room, "I've nothing to say to you."

"Well, just listen to me, then."

She gave in, and opened the door.

"How much have you had?" she asked, letting him in.

"Usual, maybe a bit more."

Brenda shut the door and walked into the kitchen, where she put the kettle on.

"You're having a coffee. Sober you up."

Pod agreed, and Brenda got to work. There was an uneasy silence, punctured only by the clinking of the silver spoon against the mug, and the steam of the kettle. Brenda stirred Pod's coffee violently, the swirling circle of milk spinning smaller, perfectly illustrating Pod's pickledness, as well as the state of play in his relationship.

"You were bang out of order tonight."

"I know. I'm sorry."

Brenda looked Pod in the eye.

"*Sorry sorry*, or *sorry so my annoying girlfriend'll get off my back*?"

"Sorry sorry. I mean it. Let me make it up to you."

"That's easy enough. I spoke to Sam the other day. He wants to go to Bliss, the gay bar. Not to get off with Toby, before you start panicking. It'll be Sam's first time there. He says he wants

152

to go and try it out, see what it's like. An experiment. Nothing heavy. And I said you and me would go along and support him."

Pause. Pod stared long and hard at his girlfriend. Things really had changed. She awaited his reaction.

"You are having a giraffe," he sputtered. Pod was not a happy man.

"I'm not, you're coming, end of story. You owe it to him. We're his closest friends, Pod."

"Seems pretty close to Toby, to me. Doesn't need us anymore."

"That's a lie."

"Stop defending him the whole time. I don't want to go to some faggot's paradise."

Brenda was livid. She picked up the coffee jar and, its lid still off, hurled the contents over her partner. Always one to give as good as he gets, Pod picked up the first thing he could find — the milk bottle — and lobbed milk in Brenda's direction. And so began another epic Brenda and Pod fight. In the past, they've poured drinks over each other and ripped clothes in fury, but this took their arguments into a new realm of imagination. And it all took place, so Brenda assures me, without so much as a grin on either of their faces. They were angry, and they meant business. The milk-sodden Brenda retaliated by chucking a bread roll at Pod, which didn't inflict much damage at all. Then Pod found the ultimate ammunition, resting in a paper bag by the sink.

Flour.

He opened up the pack and, despite Brenda's protests, began emptying it in her general direction. Brenda managed to

153

get a hand out and turn the bag round so it faced Pod, and covered him in it too. There was now a combination of coffee granules, milk, flour, and breadcrumbs covering the golden couple. Infuriated, Pod opened the fridge and chucked an egg at Brenda's head, leaving the yolk slowly trickling down her face as she threw a banana at his chest. They stood, out of breath, covered in white flour, at opposite ends of the kitchen, like a pair of wild animals eyeing their prey, waiting to see who was going to make the first move. It was Pod.

"I am not going."

"Why not?"

"I don't want to."

"Do you feel threatened?"

"Of course not."

"They won't pounce on you. They'll see you've got a girlfriend and leave you alone."

"They're called gay bars for a reason. They're for gays, and I'm not one of those."

"Those! You make them sound like an alien subspecies. Those includes one of your oldest friends, remember?"

"Sam's not gay. He says so himself."

"No, you're right, he's not. But apparently he's not straight either."

Pod flinched, turning slightly from his girlfriend.

"It's the truth," Brenda continued. "What's your problem with the truth?"

"Well, how come he never used to like boys?"

"Maybe he did, Pod, but people like you made him so petrified, so scared of rejection, he wouldn't tell a soul."

"That's not fair. I've never been nasty to him."

"I'm sorry, but you know I care about him."

Then came Pod's distraction argument. At least, that's my analysis of it. He threw in a crazy idea to shift the focus from his bigotry firmly onto Brenda.

"I know you spend a lot of time with him," he said. Brenda knew his game instantly.

"So that's it. Come on, out with it. If you're worried I'm shagging Sam, out with it."

Pod feigned shock. Brenda reminded him of his problems with honesty:

"It's what you were thinking, isn't it? What's so wrong with the truth, Pod?"

"I never thought you were shagging, I just didn't want you spending more time with him than you do with me. He's your friend, I'm your boyfriend. Lately those two terms have got a bit confused, that's all." Seems I wasn't the only one having problems with labels.

"He's going through a difficult time, Pod. He needs support, and I'm all he's got."

Very sweet of Brenda and all that, but a bit self-congratulatory.

"What about Toby, his newfound friend?" I could just imagine Pod spitting out "newfound friend."

"He's part of the difficult time."

"Yeah, well, maybe I'm going through a tricky time accepting one of my oldest friends is . . ." Pod stopped himself. If he really couldn't admit things about other people, what hope did he have for himself?

". . . not straight?" Brenda said, completing the sentence.

155

"Well, that's your problem, not his. And I want to help you with it." Good old Brenda. Despite the fact she was at Pod's throat, she offered to forgive and assist.

"I don't need help." Good old Pod. Despite the sweet offer of help, he remained stubborn and stiff-upper-lipped.

"Why do you keep it all in? What good does that do anyone?" Brenda was losing her patience again. Pod let rip, at last expressing his true views.

"All right, I'll tell you what I think. I think I'm straight, I've always liked girls. I think Oscar Wilde was gay, he always liked boys. I don't get how Sam can be both. Sounds to me like he's hedging his bets. Can't make his mind up. It's worse than just being gay, you know. It's slagging."

When Brenda told me this, I was shocked, and more than somewhat. Disapproving is one thing, but insulting is another. Pod had never dissed me with such passion and articulation as he did that night. We'd always had our spats, but they were over trivial things, and they were resolved within hours. The things he said to Brenda that night were new and frightening. It sounded as if he meant the malice, and yet I had never harmed him, never truly upset him, never given him cause to be so mean.

"But Oscar Wilde was married," riposted Brenda. Brilliant.

"You get my fucking point, Brenda," Pod lashed out.

"But you don't get mine. You used to be his best mate. You two were close."

"Didn't mean I wanted to shag him."

"Sex isn't everything, Pod. You should bloody know that. I can't even remember the last time we —" Brenda interrupted herself before causing too much damage. When she told me about this I was really surprised. I assumed she and Pod had a healthy sex relationship. In fact, until Brenda told me, I *assumed* all young couples had good intercourse regularly. I had no idea that she and Pod hadn't shagged since Christmastime. She said it just "sort of stopped happening," without any discussion or intention. Pod was too ashamed to mention it, and Brenda said that it felt right to keep sex out of it while they reevaluated their long-distance relationship.

"Why is it only shagging that defines anything?" continued Brenda, getting into her argument's stride. "Lots of gay blokes have shagged women, you know." Once again, I had no idea this happened. Well, I presumed people who did that were "bisexuals." But apparently, Brenda's gay uni mate Frank shagged a girl on campus because he felt sorry for her. I wish people slept with me for that reason.

"It's not black and white, but everyone's so bloody frightened they stick to these words — gay, straight, poof. But that's all they are. Words. Sam is finally coming to terms with what he is and the dictionary is no help to him whatsoever. And neither will you be if you carry on like this. Help him, Pod. Be his mate again. He just wants to go and try it out, see how he feels. It would mean a lot to him if you came to this bar."

"I'll try to be his mate again, I will," started Pod, and as Brenda told me this, I thought he just might be up for it.

"But I'm not going, all right?" And with that he was off out of the front door, his food-splattered figure furiously pacing the streets of Surbiton.

"What are you so scared of?" Brenda shouted after him.

I thought long and hard about all of that. Probably for an hour. Sitting on a toilet seat for an hour is not a comfortable business, although my home toilet is considerably less painful on the buttocks than a public lavatory. Nonetheless, my brain was aching as much as my butt was while I desperately tried to figure out what Pod would be like the next time we spoke, whether I should phone him, whether I should go to this bar at all. Was I ready to pull a bloke, especially with my friends there? Would old men in dark corners try to touch me? Would I get stubble rash?

One thing was for certain, however. Pod had severe problems with me, and for the first time he'd aired them coherently. The row in the pub seemed like petty bickering next to what he had said to Brenda. She was incredibly upset when we spoke, and reiterated her doubts about how much longer the relationship would last.

"Sometimes you stay with someone because it's comfortable," she said. "Because it's harder to split it up than it is to carry on. But we're becoming so different. It's funny. It used to bother me that he wouldn't open up or be honest, but now that he's beginning to tell me, I'm really not sure I like what he's saying."

It was great to have Brenda tell me her problems. Not in a bad way — it was awful that she had these sorts of dilemmas, but it just felt good that she trusted me. I wished I could have said something useful, but after what I'd just heard, I was inclined to agree and suggest she spend a period of time away from Pod. But he was still my mate, and I did have some ounces of forgiveness left in me, and I worried about him being all single and bitter. There was something so reliable and safe about

Brenda and Pod, a bit like "Our Tree," and right now, in this time of uncertainty and changes, I really didn't need another pillar of regularity being taken away from me. I think that was the subconscious reason I encouraged her to keep at it. Selfish, I suppose.

"Give it some time," I suggested. "Maybe once I've cleared up what it is I am in my head, it'll help Pod too."

CHAPTER 13

"I'M TOO SEXY FOR MY SHIRT."
— RIGHT SAID FRED

Brenda was right. I only wanted to "try it out." I had heard things about Bliss, but with her and Toby's support, I was mustering up enough courage to at least poke my head around the door and catch my first proper whiff of homosexual air. (And what air it would turn out to be.) This evening was to be a tentative first step into the undiscovered territory of unstraightness. It was supposed to help me clear up a few things in my mind, and discover whether:

a) boys were my thing,
and
b) the gay scene was my thing.

I woke up that Thursday with a real sense of apprehension, my stomach filled with tingly fear. Brenda and I had checked out the Bliss website, and figured that Thursday was the best night to go. Wednesday was transvestite night, Friday was the male stripper parade, and lately Saturdays had been put aside for the prestigious Mr. Gay South-East contest. The other bonus about Thursdays was "pound a pint" and a special "buy one, get one free" offer on tequila shots.

I spent most of the day lounging around at home, trying unsuccessfully not to think about Bliss, doing very little other than eating and watching daytime TV. Sandra from Shrewsbury had chosen a nationwide TV chat show to announce to her husband, Troy, that she was leaving him for another woman. Troy's sister Dervla, in fact. This upset Troy so much that he had been forced to make an announcement of his own; he had been having an affair with Sandra's mother, Annette, for the last two years. Sitting next to me on the couch, enjoying her day off work, my mum told me that, once upon a time, British people were too scared to even have a row on the streets for fear of causing a scene. Nowadays it seems that if we don't cause a scene we're being abnormal. In fact, causing a scene is a bonus because it makes us a bit famous and there's always the possibility of an autobiography (which has actually been written by a clever person) or, better still, a DIY TV show. In any case, all this weird incestuous sex was making me nervous. Fortunately, my mum put on a DVD she had just bought — *The Greatest "Neighbours" Weddings of All Time*. Basically, a bunch of marital specials from the hugely popular Australian soap opera. I sat by her as she sobbed her way through Scott (Jason Donovan) and Charlene (Kylie Minogue)'s famous wedding scene.

"Mum!" I exclaimed, embarrassed.

"Sam, this is important."

"How the hell is a tacky old soap wedding important?"

"You're too cynical. Romance is alive and well," she said, sobbing further into her tissue. "And it's so swe-e-e-et," she mumbled.

I felt sorry for my mum. Fate had dealt her a nasty blow with marriage to my dad. She was obviously wanting something more. At fifty, she is still very much in with a chance of meeting a new fella, but I think she's found contentment in line-dancing, cooking great pork chops, and watching *Greatest "Neighbours" Weddings of All Time.* Each to their own. But I didn't like to see her cry, whatever the occasion. I put a consoling arm around her.

When Scott and Charlene finally kissed, now man and wife, Mum went off on one, crying uncontrollably for what seemed like an eternity. This did nothing for my nerves, so I arranged to meet Brenda for a swift few down at the Church and Abbey before we set off for Bliss.

I've always taken care with what I wear, but on this particular night I spent about half an hour in front of the mirror choosing potential garb. I think nerves took over, and my indecision was beginning to piss me off. I'm good on color coordination, or so I think, so it was obvious my bright and, frankly, camp red T-shirt wouldn't work with my green combat trousers. The tight-fitting *Knight Rider* T-shirt — a cartoon of David Hasselhoff leaning on his black vehicle — was far too gay. I didn't want to come across as camp, I wanted to come across as me.

It was six o'clock, torrential rain was tapping angrily against the windows, I had no idea what to wear, and I was beginning to have serious doubts. I phoned Brenda again.

"Brenda, I can't go through with it. This is stupid. I *feel* stupid."

"Shut up. I've had the biggest row of my life with Pod over

this and you're coming whether you like it or not. See you at the Abbey in forty-five."

With that, she hung up.

I stood in the middle of my bedroom, dressed in only my boxer shorts and socks, the portable phone still pressed to my ear. That was the first time she'd ever done that. But she was absolutely right. I was going whether I liked it or not. I chose the black jeans and blue short-sleeve shirt, waxed my hair to look presentable, massaged in some face moisturizer to get rid of the dry skin, and eyed myself in the mirror. Every now and then, when you've gone to a little effort, or even when you haven't, you can't help but feel good at what you see in the mirror. *I most definitely fancy me*, I thought. With a spring in my step, and a confidence in my head, I picked up my keys, wallet, and mobile phone, and headed off, telling Mum no truths.

"Off to Brenda's . . . probably not back till the morning," I said. She waved me off, and I noticed she was watching Scott and Charlene's wedding again. No tears this time.

The Abbey was fairly empty. Brenda told me she and Pod hadn't spoken since the food fight. I told her more about the aquarium trip, and how Toby made me feel.

"Looks as if we've both been hanging around insensitive blokes, doesn't it?" she said.

"D'you think he was out of order?" I asked, craving some advice.

"Yes, I do. But maybe it just didn't cross his mind that the way he was behaving might upset you."

I paused for thought. "He's not stupid," I said.

"Clever people can be insensitive too," she said. "Look, from what you've told me, he's a sound guy. He's probably having a

163

hard time with things. Give him a chance." Brenda was always anxious to find the good in other people, which I guessed was becoming a very hard task with her own boyfriend.

"Brenda . . ."

"Sam . . ."

"Is he keeping me down? Should I stop being his friend?"

"D'you think you'd have been so honest about yourself if you hadn't met Toby?"

"I s'pose not. But —"

"Precisely. I think he's a good bloke, Sam. The way he looked after you when you barfed your guts up in London . . . he cares. Give him a chance."

The levelheaded advice left me feeling warm and excited. After a few pints of Dutch courage, during which Brenda seemed decidedly off-color and down, I found myself cheering her up for the first time in ages. She responds quickly to a bit of interest from others, and once I'd told her how much tonight meant to me, she seemed to be nearing top form again. We left for Bliss, walking the twenty-minutes-or-so journey hand in hand. Brenda and I hadn't held each other's hands since we were about thirteen. It felt so right, and so harmless. We were friends, and I loved her.

It was only nine o'clock but there was already a nasty queue outside the club. Thankfully, the relentless rain had finally stopped. After a few minutes, Toby and Lucy arrived. They were careful not to look like a couple in case the bouncer refused them entry on the grounds of being too straight. I was quite pleased at their restraint, because I was in no mood for a twenty-minute close-up view of the happy couple being . . . happy.

Brenda and Toby began chatting about nothing in particular, but they did it quite well, which left me awkwardly next to Lucy, aware that one of us should break the ice.

"I hear your mate's being an arse . . . ?" she started. I presumed she meant Pod and not Toby.

"Pod? Yeah, well, he's having a hard time, I think. Always been a bit of a tough nut to crack, has Pod."

"Well, he certainly sounds like a nut," she said with a chuckle. Crap gag. I smiled lamely, and we resumed our silence. It's amazing how long you can spend examining your shoes when you can't make conversation. I decided my black loafers could have done with a polish.

Fortunately, the queue moved pretty quickly. I looked nervously at everybody else, in front and behind. No one looked especially gay, apart from a guy around twenty-five who had a white T-shirt tightly protecting his pecs and biceps like a plate of armor. Urgh. There were loads of fag hags, most of them wearing far too much makeup and carrying kitsch handbags. I did keep catching the eye of one young guy about my age, with a huge nose and beady little eyes. His T-shirt was the most unattractive thing about him, though: a copy of the Coca-Cola logo, but it said something else instead of Enjoy Coke.

As we neared the front, my heart began beating faster and faster. I could never have managed this by myself, so I made it clear how grateful I was to Brenda (and Toby) for accompanying me. The bouncer was surprisingly straight, with a hard, ugly face and rugby-player body.

"Evening. You're aware this is a gay club, yes?" he asked. *How polite*, I thought. We nodded.

"Are you together?" he asked, meaning the four of us.

"Yeah, it's our anniversary night . . . one month," said Toby, taking my hand in his.

Blimey. I wasn't ready for that. I began seeing all wobbly. The bouncer became a faceless jelly wrapped up in a tuxedo. Brenda turned into a blob. My eyes watered a bit. What did he say that for? Brenda's and Lucy's giggles seemed to go on forever, piercing my eardrums with an offensive and mocking loudness. Bastard. He knew I was messed up over him. *Everything's a game to Toby*, I thought. Why couldn't he take me seriously? And he had made obvious his complete lack of proper feelings for me by ridiculing the possibility that we could be a couple. Double bastard.

The bouncer hurried us along, we paid our very reasonable entry fee to the craggy thirtysomething at the till, and descended the neon-lit stairway into Bliss. Sped-up pop played — mainly remixes of some classic cheesy tunes. This was everything I'd heard the gay scene to be, and more. There were posters lining the stairway. In between one that advertised a *Special, one-off performance by Desiree Maxwell* (who she?) and another that promoted a *School uniform night for naughty boys*, there were posters about Hepatitis A and B vaccines.

The bar was heaving. It was far bigger than I expected — a huge dance floor at one end, with a mirror floor and several mirror balls above it. The DJ was in a booth hanging from the ceiling, just above the tallest dancers. At this point, there weren't many people boogying, although the area around the bar, at the opposite end of the dance floor, was packed. Dotted about were several small, red tables and chairs, and numerous little booths where you could go to hide in the dark and, presumably, get up to mischief. We made a beeline for the bar and stuck together.

I have to admit I felt a bit scared, but not threatened. The first thing I noticed was how all eyes were turning to stare at me, and at Toby, as though we were being displayed for sale at the local market, which in a way we were. I remember thinking I knew what it must feel like to be a girl going into a straight pub or club, surrounded by salivating blokes desperate for a bit of it. I was particularly miffed at the number of "older gentlemen" in Bliss. A third of the crowd was definitely over forty. This worried me. Didn't they have homes to go to? Books to read? Or would that be mc — washed up, wrinkly, and desperate for a shag at forty-eight? I should hope not! There was one particular fortysomething who, while I was at the bar getting the cheap drinks in, kept nudging me. In turn, I kept ignoring him. After a while (there were only three barmen for about two hundred punters, so the wait was lengthy) I couldn't ignore his constant staring any longer. I looked back.

He was shocking. Extremely well-built, extremely tanned, extremely extreme in every respect. He smiled, showing his extremely white teeth. His crow's feet were like a cluster of canals flowing into the eyeballs. He was old. Years of sunbed abuse were taking their toll on his complexion.

"Rob," he said. What makes these people think we'd be interested? How dare he even think someone like me would go for something like him? Dirty slapper. I was too scared to give him my real name, so without much thought I answered with a lie.

"Alex," I said, and looked back towards the bar. Suddenly, his hand was in my hair. What was this? An orgy? Did I give

167

him any suggestion whatsoever that I was interested in him? I turned to find Brenda, but she and the others had nabbed a booth and sat down. They were meters away. I was on my own, and the resolve built within me.

"What are you doing?" I asked.

"Your hair's lovely," he said. "I love it here. It's so chilled out. But you know what I can't stand?" he asked, removing his hand from my hair.

"What?" I replied, with deliberate curtness.

"Promiscuous blokes. So many of 'em. Makes me sick." I couldn't quite believe this. Suddenly, a slight Chinese man, only about twenty, popped up, seemingly from nowhere. He stood next to Rob.

"Oh, Alex, meet Ming."

"Hi," I said, and shook the ultra-limp hand. Ming didn't say anything. But he did whisper into Rob's ear, and Rob smiled.

"Ming's a fashion assistant," said Rob, and I wondered how low down the fashion scale that really was. Does he make coffee? Sew buttons? Tend to models' sexual desires for a price? "And he reckons you have the schoolboy look. You could make it."

This was getting far too cheesy, and clearly Rob was getting off on me potentially looking like a schoolboy. I wasn't about to let him be my teacher, so I smiled politely and turned away. Fortunately, he got the message and pissed off.

I joined the others in the booth. They chuckled when I told them of my misfortune. We made casual banter, listened to the music, watched the dancers dance and the kissers kiss. Bliss seemed a lot more urgent than an ordinary club; there was more passion, more speed, more action. Hands fumbled all around, wriggling underneath shirts and belts. I found it all quite exciting, and realized that, despite what people say, we're not all the same. Most gay people aren't like most straight people. There seemed to be no gray area in coupling off; once you pulled, you got yourself a shag. With girls, it's never a foregone conclusion. And often you don't want it to be. In here, two guys would get it on and within minutes they were out the door.

I wonder if the cause of all this rush, of this slaggishness, is because these guys can't really be themselves outside of the four safe walls of a gay bar. Outside, in the real world, they'd probably be beaten shitless if they chatted someone up at the bus stop, or the supermarket, or ice rink. A straight bloke can be himself anywhere and, despite the fear of crashing and burning, at least he won't be attacked for acting on his feelings. Not so for unstraight folk. It's just not an option to approach the boy you fancy at the bus stop, you have to keep it all inside, and that gets kinda crazy sometimes. I guess it all just explodes when you're in a safe haven like Bliss. I mean, all blokes think with their dicks, so when two dick-led beings get together it's going to be chaotic.

After a while Lucy and Toby got a bit closer, holding hands under the table and kissing when no bouncers or bar staff walked past. I felt decidedly uncomfortable about this, so I grabbed Brenda and we stood by the dance floor, watching in silence for a while. Ultra Naté's "Free" boomed on the speakers, and I thought of the chorus.

You're free to do what you want to do
You've got to live your life, do what you want to do

I couldn't help thinking that, although I'd come this far, I still wasn't free.

It was midnight. I had already downed a lot of cheap booze, and I was displeased about the Rob incident, and starting to get angry with Toby. I lashed out in Brenda's direction.

"Look at the slags," I started. "Tight T-shirt himbos . . . you don't find love in a place like this. You don't find anything meaningful. Why did we come here? I hate it here."

"Stop whinging, at least you're getting sharked. Take a look — everyone's staring at you. Look over there, blond lad, by himself. Tongue hanging out of his mouth."

She was right. There was a really young guy, all on his own, leaning against the wall. He wore a Kylie Minogue T-shirt and stonewashed jeans (memories of the *Neighbours* wedding came flooding back . . .). I waved politely at him, before switching the wave into a middle-finger salute, adding a mimed "fuck off" for full aggressive effect. I projected *Come and have a go if you think you're hard enough* vibes. His smile melted and he turned away.

"Will you chill out?" shouted Brenda. "Blimey, at least you've got a gay bar. Think of the poor faggot living in Redcar —"

"Where's Redcar?" I asked.

"I don't know, but it's miles away from anywhere."

Fair point, well made. But I still wasn't happy.

"A forty-year-old pervert and a fifteen-year-old dickhead. This is not what I call a successful evening. Look at the fucking poster," I said, reading out the huge banner across the DJ booth. "'Bring your mobile phones to use as electronic slag tags.' I hate this. Let's get pissed, come on." I grabbed Brenda by the hand and ran to the bar, barging past people and generally behaving like a bit of a dick. But I felt I was justified in my dick-ishness.

Toby has since told me that, while Brenda and I left them to it, rather than spend the entire time snogging and feeling each other up, they had a chat about me. Lucy, bless her, was concerned. Toby reckoned all I needed was a shag, but she thought I fancied him. She also described me as "low and vulnerable," which I think was meant to be sympathetic. She even wondered if I had an ulterior motive for bringing Toby to the club, with my actual plan being to pull him. That was total bollocks, but at least she cared. Toby explained that he and I were "intimate friends," apparently. Brenda, meanwhile, was telling me off.

"Sam, I don't want you to get hammered tonight," she demanded. Bit late for that.

"Why the buggery bollocks not?" I asked.

"It won't help. But . . . but coming out will."

There was a shivery pause. She'd never been this blunt over the issue of me telling people about my predicament.

"I'm not gay. I don't need to come out."

"No, OK, you're not gay," she reasoned, "but you're not straight either. You'd feel a lot better if you told people. As many people as you can."

"Bollocks, no one will understand." I gulped a mouthful of watered-down beer. "And if you're saying that, you don't understand either."

The DJ switched from upbeat to slowbeat — 10CC's "I'm Not in Love." The lights turned cold blue, caking us in their icy glare so that we all looked like something out of a sci-fi movie. Smoke machines hissed and filled the dance floor with a thick mist, turned blue by the lights. Brenda tried to grab my glass, but I fought her off. After a few bars of the song, Toby appeared from the blackness of the booth, hand in hand with Lucy. Suddenly they were being very public about their relationship. Weird how the tables were turned. In here, they were the minority, and they provoked more than a few frowns.

The happy couple started slow-dancing to the cheese-fest that is "I'm Not in Love." Brenda and I stood nearby, watching. Well, in my case, staring. Glaring. Fascinated. The blue light made Toby's face look angelic and beautiful and special. Out of this world.

And he was dancing with someone else. For the first time, I admitted to myself I wanted him. I wanted that dance. Nothing more, just that dance. Our eyes locked, and I didn't look away. We must have been eyeing each other, his face neutral and mine probably full of upset, for about ten seconds. He *must* have known I was jealous.

It was something so simple — a little dance. But I wanted it so badly. It was sweet, romantic, and lovely, and I'd never experienced those things with another person. Maybe my mum was right — romance *was* alive and well.

The moment was interrupted by the supercamp DJ:

"Bit of a dance floor emptier that one . . . sorry, babes! How about this 80s cheese classic? Slice of Brie for the chickens and twinks!" He then proceeded to impersonate a chicken and play Cyndi Lauper's "Girls Just Wanna Have Fun." I grabbed Lucy and started dancing with her like some sort of ecstasy-popping maniac. She joined in with a smile, but Toby wasn't happy.

"All right, mate. Come on, you've had a bit too much," he said, referring to the booze, but he could easily have been talking about his girlfriend.

"Sod that," I shouted. "The night is still young, and I'm sick of those forty-year-old mongs feeling me up —"

"Leave her alone, Sam," said Toby, with a threatening tone.

"It's OK, Toby," said Lucy, keeping the peace.

I went to Toby, expecting a hug, and he stepped back. I was pissed, so the hurt was exaggerated.

"I thought you wanted to meet someone," he said.

"I'm busy. Piss off."

"What's your problem?" he asked.

Summoning the nasty energy from some unexplored bit of my body, I pushed him with a "Just piss off, will you?" and I felt this uncontrollable anger whizzing up through me. I was firing.

Brenda stepped in, standing between the two of us in an attempt to pacify.

Lucy pitched in. "Sam, calm down, we don't need to get —"

But Toby interrupted her before she could go on. "Just tell me what the problem is," he pleaded.

I stared at him again. We made eye contact, but it couldn't have been more different from the 10CC moment. There was anger in our eyes. It felt awful.

"You're the problem. I wish I'd never met you."

And I meant it. I ran out of the club.

CHAPTER 14

LEARNING TO DANCE

I stormed up the stairs and past the bouncers. There was still a healthy queue outside.

"Don't fucking bother," I shouted at the hopeful clubbers. A mincey guy, about thirty, stared at me as I walked purposefully past the line.

"*Some*one's having a queeny fit," he said to a friend.

"Shut up, you stupid poof," I said.

I instantly felt ashamed. I didn't mean to abuse him like that. I guess it just kind of came out. He was stunned into silence, and I ran as fast as I could to the town center, where I sought solace in the late-night Paradiso Grill, serving the "best kebabs and burgers in Surrey." A gang of young teenage kids always assembled outside it on weekend nights, usually to smoke, spit, drink cider, and try out break-dance moves. White, black, Asian — the kids were united. I walked right through their dance routines into the fast-food joint, where I ordered a milk shake and headed straight for the toilet, only to find an

Out of Order sign dangling on the door, which mysteriously appeared every night at around ten. The place was virtually empty, apart from a couple of pissed old geezers arguing over the price of a cheeseburger, and a bunch of tracksuited thirteen-year-olds talking loudly and listening to one another's mobile phone ring tones.

I plonked myself down at one of those off-yellow, plasticy tables and, as ever, I thought. I thought about this new side to Toby I had witnessed. About Lucy, and her good looks. About Brenda's loyalty. About them all probably bitching about me and calling me a dufus. And after only a minute or two of all this worrying, in walked Greg. I didn't know he was Greg when he came in, but I found out soon after, when he sat opposite me at my table.

"Do I know you?" I asked him, the alcohol encouraging my cheek.

"I was in the queue at Bliss." Ah. He was going to kick the shit out of me.

"Oh. You're pissed off about what I said."

"No. In fact I was going to agree with you. He *is* a stupid poof."

I couldn't help but chuckle. This guy seemed all right. Not at all camp, quite good-looking, but a lot older. Probably a little over thirty. He was well-built, but not in a beefy, gym kind of way. Just naturally a stout guy, with green eyes and good skin. I was a little uneasy in his presence; who exactly was he, and why did he follow me?

"I'm Greg," he said, and I told him my name. My real name, this time.

"Don't freak out," he continued. "I'm not stalking you. I

175

gave up on that queue after you left, hadn't moved an inch in half an hour. I was passing by the High Street, saw you here and . . . well, thought I'd say hello." I looked neutrally at him, almost through him. "I can go, if you'd prefer to be alone," he said.

"No, you're all right," I replied.

"You seemed a bit pissed off back there. Boyfriend dump you?"

"I don't have a boyfriend."

"Oh? So what griped you?"

"Just . . . stuff."

"Oh, stuff. I know what you mean. I have stuff problems too."

I couldn't help but smile.

"What do you do?" I asked him.

"I'm a firefighter."

"Firefighter? Blimey." I looked a little surprised.

"Yeah, these gayboys get everywhere nowadays, don't we? You are gay, I take it?"

"Er . . . well, thing is I don't — " I saw him smirk, rather smugly, and I stopped myself.

"What?" I asked him.

"Nothing, it's fine. What are you, eighteen?"

"Nineteen," I said.

"You're still a bit confused, then," he said, very matter-of-factly.

"Don't patronize," I said.

"Sorry, I didn't mean to." He sat back in his seat, his big hands sitting on the table.

"So are you?"

"Am I what?

"Gay?"

"I can be," I said, pleased with the air of mystery. Greg just looked annoyingly wise and seen-it-all-before. I asked him if he had a boyfriend. He explained that he didn't, that he'd been single for two years, and that he didn't fancy any of the blokes in Bliss. He preferred venturing up into London's Soho when he could. I explained about my Soho experience, and he laughed and winced. We began chatting about all sorts — he told me about the fire brigade, I told him about college. After the hassles of the night, it was quite calming to speak with a complete stranger. We didn't talk about relationships, sexuality or sex, preferring to stick to jobs, careers, and the crapness of local nightlife. Greg had few gay friends locally, so he often went to Bliss by himself. I thought he was brave. Until recently, there was no way I'd have told a random bloke all about my true self, but here I was telling him about the Rangers and the Summer Cup. He wished me luck. Then there was a pause in the conversation. I sucked up the last of my vanilla milk shake, making that awful slurpy noise with my straw. I noticed the dead quiet around us, the old geezers having fallen asleep, and the ring tone kids having left. The two Greek men who ran the joint were watching, but I didn't really care.

"Is everything all right?" he asked, with a genuinely sympathetic tone.

"Fine, why wouldn't it be?"

"Well, earlier . . . you were upset. If it's not your boyfriend, what is it?"

I found myself explaining the entire sorry mess to the poor guy. For about ten minutes. He didn't get a word in edgeways as I recounted how Toby and I had both admitted being "gentle," and how the beautiful Lucy had come along and destroyed our balance. When you're feeling low and pissed, you'll tell anybody anything. But Greg wasn't just anybody — well, he was, but he was a good kind of anybody. I liked him. He liked me.

"Pretty big mess, huh?" he said.

"Yeah. But it's my own fault. I'm to blame."

"That's big of you to admit. But I reckon you should be talking to Toby. Sort things out. Whaddya reckon?"

"I reckon you're right. Is it too late to go over now?"

"No time like the present. I can't say I've ever been in your shoes, but sounds to me like you should chill out a bit. Not take things so seriously. Go with the flow. There, I'm all out of cheesy phrases. But you get my point . . . don't worry so much about yourself. Easier said than done, I know."

"You're very kind," I said, sounding like a bit of a wuss. "Listening to me banging on, you're a patient sod, aren't ya? I mean it, though . . . thanks."

"You're welcome."

I got up to leave. But I kind of wanted to stay and talk to this guy some more.

"You know I haven't been trying to chat you up, don't you?" he said.

"Yeah, course I knew. Honest!"

"Everyone thinks we're all out for just one thing."

"Yeah, well most of us are." I used "us" without realizing, but I made no effort to correct myself. It felt right and truthful and, above all, honest. I couldn't identify with gay, particularly not the Bliss type of gay, but I felt I could identify with Greg.

"I suppose you're right. It's all a bit daunting. Tonight was

178

your first night in a gay bar, wasn't it?" I nodded. He didn't say it condescendingly or jokingly, he was just being . . . well, being nice.

"I'll never forget my first time, by myself, in Southampton," he continued. "I was a well skinny, spotty twenty-year-old. Worst ten minutes of my life."

I laughed. He was so easy to get along with, unassuming and, at the same time, confident. I had to ask him —

"Can I take your number? In a friends-only sense, that is."

He smiled, agreed, and noted it down on a bright and brash Bliss flyer, with *Electronic Slag Tags* in large bold type across the top. I shoved it in my pocket and thanked him again for his time.

"Call me if you fancy going to Bliss, maybe together we'll be able to stomach it," he said. He stayed seated as I made to leave. But it didn't feel quite right, I felt like I owed him something more. Although I still felt shit about the Toby situation, he'd made me feel happier and I wanted to show him how much I liked him. In a friends-only way. I didn't fancy this guy at all, but he was patient, funny, and had charm. He was a lot of good things, but above all he was a grown-up. He seemed level-headed, experienced, and able to look at us youngsters with a degree of affectionate cynicism and sardonic humor. I appreciated all of that. After the disastrous Rob, the bizarre Ming, and the tight T-shirts, it was such a relief to meet an ordinary, easy-going guy. So I sat down again, and in a moment of unplanned oddness, put two fingers to my lips and then placed them on his cheek, quick-as-you-like. He smiled at me and did the same back. I didn't even check to see if we were being watched. I made sure his number was still in my pocket, then left, joining the throng of break-dancing kids outside. And I was still feeling pretty good, having successfully pushed Toby to the back of my mind, albeit temporarily. So I cockily went up to the dancers and asked them to teach me a few moves. In what was turning out to be the weirdest night of the weirdest summer in my weird life, they invited me into their circle. I was with it. Word.

CHAPTER 15

"SUDDENLY YOU'RE HEARING ME,
SO I'M TALKING JUST AS FAST AS I CAN."
— ANGRY ANDERSON

"That boy can be an absolute tit-face sometimes," was Brenda's response to my hasty exit from Bliss.

My memory of events is a little hazy, but to the best of my knowledge, it went something like this: At about 4:30 in the morning, I went over to Toby's, holding a half-empty bottle of Pinot Grigio I'd nicked from my mum's supply. And yes, half empty, not half full. Greg notwithstanding, this was definitely a night for pessimism. Toby answered the door in his dressing gown, his eyes caked in sleep, his hair an unwieldy mess. He didn't look like Toby. He looked a lot less handsome, and half as cocky.

"Where the hell did you go? Come in, you look like a pissed tramp."

He wasn't wrong. I'd ripped my jeans on the park bench I'd dozed on and my hair was ruffled. I stepped in.

"Is she here?" I inquired.

"Lucy," he said, pausing as if to say I was being rude in calling her "she," ". . . is at home. You ruined the evening. Where did you go?"

"I . . . learned how to break-dance with some kids outside Paradiso Grill," I answered. This was a half-truth. After the dance jam, I went to the park, slept on the bench, grabbed some wine from home, and came right to Toby's.

I approached him for a hug, but he wasn't interested. Again. "Why not?" I asked.

"You know why not." I wasn't sure that I did. "You're gonna have to face up to it sooner or later," he said.

"Face up to what?"

"Your problem. If you won't tell me, tell Brenda, tell someone. . . ."

I sat on his couch and sipped from the wine.

"It's no big deal. . . . You got a glass?" I said.

He ignored my question. "I'd say it's a great big obese deal. You're jealous."

"I am not," I protested.

"You're jealous of what Lucy's got."

It hit home. He knew I was into him.

"Don't flatter yourself."

"Don't fool yourself. We're still friends, you know. That hasn't changed. But I enjoy Lucy's company and I like going out with her."

"You'll never understand me. Nobody does, you're all just conforming. Doing what's expected." This was drunken rambling, but I did think no one understood me, and I was pondering whether Toby was really brave at all. He liked to joke, and aggravate, and play on people's fears, but this was the guy who ended a relationship with another guy because he couldn't be public about it. Was he being chicken now, going for the easy option — trophy Lucy?

"What the fuck do you know?" I asked. "You've got it easy."

He looked at me hard. "Don't say that."

"Why not? It's true. You live away from home. I don't. Your dad never walked out on you. Mine did."

I really meant that last bit. I felt hard done-by, but I also felt like a twat if I went on about it. I was always taught to remember how lucky I really was. And yet, in this drunken moment of honesty, I told him exactly what I thought, expressing years of resentment. He wasn't a happy bunny.

"Don't say that. Don't ever say that," he shouted. "You don't know what you're talking about. You think life's a bed of roses for me, don't you? You ever tried living with my dad? You've never even met him. You might know about me, but if he ever found out, if he heard a whisper that I'd been with guys, he'd disown me. No arguments, he'd never speak to me again. I couldn't even give Paul my phone number, I was so shit scared Dad would work out what was going on. I lied every time I went out, telling him I was just going to a friend's house. He's a bastard and I've never had it easy."

There was real passion in his voice, an anger that I felt flattered to have incited, in a way. That sounds daft, but at this point in the summer, our relationship seemed to inspire either moments of warm tenderness or complete fury, and I quite enjoyed that. I carried on the angry theme of the night with a quick riposte:

"We all have to lie, Toby. You're nothing special."

183

He'd saved the worst bit till last.

"I thought about topping myself, OK? Really thought about it. At school. I'd had enough. Nobody knew about me, I was totally alone, I hated myself. What would you know about real fear? Fear of rejection like the fear I feel."

I was surprised to hear how low Toby could fall. He always seemed too ice-cool, too in control of things to be capable of real depression. But I'd overestimated him. Clearly school was as much of a struggle for him as it was for me, or even more so, given that he had a fella on the go.

But I was in an argumentative mood.

"Don't tell me I don't know fear of rejection —" I started, but he was feeling really vicious now.

"Your dad's not around, your mum doesn't give two shits about you."

I felt that sick feeling. "Take that back, Toby."

"It's true, she couldn't care less —"

"Don't you dare insult my mum, you arsehole. Take that back now."

"No, it's about time someone told you the truth."

"Fuck off." I pushed him backwards.

"Fuck off yourself."

And he shoved me to the floor. He came over to help me up, seemingly apologetic, but I was having none of it. I pushed him, he fell backwards and I wrestled, keeping him on the floor. We were in the middle of a full-blown scrap; I went to punch him, he grabbed my hand and punched me in the stomach, winding me. Short of breath, I kneed him in his tummy and he keeled over. We both got to our feet and continued grappling with each other's arms, before I gave up and held him tight. I stopped moving. Then the crying started. Uncontrollably. I hadn't cried like this since the night of the school dance, over a year previously. I wanted to stop, but couldn't, and it frightened me.

"I'm sorry. Please don't let go," I said, not really knowing where this sudden peace had come from.

"It's all right. You're all right now, Sam. I'm sorry too."

We stayed hugging for ages — a minute or two — in total silence, apart from the sound of my sobs. It felt good, although my stomach still ached from the violence earlier.

We didn't say much more that night. Toby got me a blanket and pillow and I lay down on the couch. All I could hear was the hypnotic buzz of the fridge, which formed a surreal soundtrack to the spinning, blurred, and side-on visuals in front of me, until eventually I fell into a drunken slumber.

Later that morning, at about 9:30, I was awoken by Toby opening the curtains and letting the bright sun into the living room. I stirred, making strange animal-like noises. I am not a morning person.

"I was slaughtered, wasn't I? Last night's a bit of a blur," I said. Toby sat on the back of the couch, looking down at me, a mug of hot tea in his hand. I could smell the booze on me.

"Did anything . . . ? I mean, did you . . . you know . . . I mean, what happened?" I asked, genuinely confused and lost. I'm not at my sharpest when I've just woken up.

"Don't worry, Sam. It's all fine."

He put his hand on mine briefly and smiled down at me.

"You're quite sweet when you sleep."

Blimey! That was like a honeymoon night husband-to-wife comment.

"I have to say," he continued, "it's pretty special watching someone get lost in themselves."

"What you on about? How was I lost?"

"Come on, we'll be late for football." He left for the kitchen.

CHAPTER 16

"DAMN IT, I SAID I WON'T HAVE IT THIS WAY."
— THE WANNADIES

The last thing I wanted that morning was training. Just hours after my first gay bar experience, my first attempted seduction by another bloke, and my first major bust-up with Toby, I was expected to play football with enthusiasm and skill. All those factors, plus the awesome amount of alcohol still pumping around my veins, ensured that I wasn't on best form at the park for this extra weekday session Harry had arranged.

Matters weren't helped by the conversation amongst the lads. All except Pretty Boy, who was mysteriously absent, were seated on the grass. Toby and I arrived a bit late, and boots were already being put on, laces tied, and socks pulled up. I was worried that comments would be made. Did Mikey know where we had been the night before? Did he tell anybody?

The chat was bad, but it wasn't that bad. The topic was infamous team groupie and easy shag, Melinda. I'd always stayed clear of her, although she would have gladly given me a servicing on numerous occasions. She had been round most the team, apart from married Trevor and Pretty Boy Pete, who never stayed around long enough to meet her properly, although rumor has it she is still desperate to shag him. Nathan the keeper was leading the praise.

"Melinda . . . fucking nice pair on her."

"How long has she been coming down here?" asked Toby.

"She's been 'active' on the team for two years now. I've had her so many times I've lost count," replied Laid Back.

"How do you know her?" Toby continued.

"She just came to a few games, hung out afterwards, and made it her main aim in life to get around the whole team," explained Chopper Chubby.

The lads laughed. I looked at Toby, who rolled his eyes. We must have looked as uncomfortable as we felt. I was dreading the inevitable.

"You've never been with her, have you, Sam?" Nathan asked me.

"Nah, not my type. Besides, I don't want your sloppy seconds, lads. They say saliva sticks around in the gob for six months," I said, to a few titters. I was so not in the mood for this dialogue, but the others were drooling with excitement. I began thinking of the "Happy Hour" lyrics.

"She's dirty, man," was Nathan's illuminating contribution to the Melinda sex discussion.

The lads were treating her like a shank of pork, a slab of beef, a chicken breast, but then her behavior hardly challenged this perception. As I sat there listening to the crudeness, Melinda struck me as strangely similar to those gay men I'd encountered the night before.

"Right, shut your traps and get warmed up," Harry hollered. Just then, the sun hid behind thick, fluffy clouds, never to reappear that day. In fact, rain began to pound down soon after. Harry has negative powers even he isn't aware of. He looked over at where Toby and I stood.

"Morning, girls," he said, and then grinned at Morph.

Bastard.

Chopper Chubby and Nathan laughed at Harry's "joke." I felt all angry inside. Toby just let it go. The most frustrating thing was the feeling of helplessness, of wanting to do something but being forced to feel completely impotent by the situation. I refused to get in a strop, because I didn't want Harry to have the satisfaction. Nor did I want to quit the team and give up the one thing I really loved, but it was so tempting to jack it in then and there. The taunting was already hurting, and given my state of mind, I wasn't sure I could take much more of it. Giving up football was something I'd never even considered before then, but suddenly it seemed like a realistic option, a way out of the stress.

I was still mildly drunk, and feeling shaky about the previous night's events, as we embarked on the mundane training exercises. Harry was visibly more nervous, with the big game less than a week away. His fingernails had been chewed to nothingness, and Morph was feeling the edginess too; he seemed to be sneezing nonstop through the session.

I was edgy too. I felt completely lost, and was on the receiving end of several Harry bollockings. Chopper's suspicious eyes continued to scan Toby, and occasionally me, and even Trevor seemed to be in a strange mood around us. The more I noticed the others looking uncomfortable, the worse it made me feel and the less focused I was on the football. I tried to guess at what sort of banter occurred before Toby and I had arrived for training. I imagined what Harry had told the others. I became more and more pissed off, and found it almost impossible to concentrate as the hard rain began to fall.

My mind was going in all sorts of directions. I felt angry that Harry had led the teasing, and frustrated that my teammates were being so quietly offensive. If they had a problem, they should just come out and say it, rather than keep silent and look at me and Toby like we were a pair of rapists. As with the last session, the end couldn't come too soon for me. I was desperate to get down the pub and down a few lunchtime shooters to try to forget. I was beginning to feel truly fed up with my lot, in a way I hadn't done before. Each time I vented my anger on the poor football with a powerful shot, it would fly miles wide. My number of shots-on-goal was well below Trevor's, and that sucked. The hard rain turned to light drizzle, and Harry folded away his enormous yellow golfing umbrella that managed to comfortably protect both him and his assistant.

We finished off with a new warming-down program, which Harry had designed all by himself. Unfortunately, he said we were all "a load of cack," particularly Laid Back Steve King, who quite calculatedly did the moves in the wrong order to throw everybody else out of sync. To everyone's surprise, Harry and Morph demonstrated the "proper" way of doing it.

Still donning his thick sheepskin coat, Harry began the latest complex technique to relax our muscles after the aches and strains of a game. It consisted of heading a ball repeatedly, quick jogs, calf muscle stretches, and, most funny of all, lying on the grass and cycling an imaginary midair bicycle. By the end of this routine, Harry looked to be just a few meters from heaven's door, his face having gone tomato red and his normally pristine, ultra-still hair looking three sheets to the wind. Slimline Morph coped a lot better. We gave a spontaneous ripple of applause — apart, of course, from Laid Back, who was busy lighting his cigarette.

"Now that's what I'm looking for," shouted Harry, clapping his hands. He bent over to catch his breath.

"That's easy for you two, you haven't been playing football for an hour," said Mikey, provocative as usual.

"Bloody useless, son," said Harry, still clinging on for dear life.

"Wrong attitude. This Cup . . . you do want to win it, Michael?" asked Morph.

"I stand to win two hundred smackers if we win, course I wanna win it," Mikey replied, as any hope that he wanted to lift the Cup out of a sense of pride and belonging went right out the window.

Trevor, who was now off the pitch and so reverted to his peaceful, intelligent tone, spoke up.

"With all due respect, I don't see you guys out there getting your heels stuck in."

Harry was incensed. "I've got my FA Coaching badges, son. I am the manager —"

"And I'm the number two," continued Morph. "We don't get stuck in, we shout. So listen up!"

"I'm just saying, give us a little break," concluded Trevor.

Harry saw nothing inappropriate in calling someone twelve years his senior *son*. In fact, he did it again.

"I wanna win, son." Harry was off again. "I want our name on that Cup. I want the Rangers to win that Cup."

I was enjoying this argument. It took the focus firmly away from me and I watched it with relish.

"Winning takes work!" Morph shouted.

Harry moved over to Toby. "And about this playing in the hole . . . all well and good, all very foreign, continental, but your hole seems to be about twenty meters wide. I mean, you're playing all over the shop. Exactly how big is this hole?"

I couldn't resist the temptation. It was too sweet an opportunity. I don't quite know how I got the courage, but I guess I was feeling so furious it was one of those nothing-to-lose situations where you just go for broke. I was proud of my Toby-esque display of defiance:

"I think Toby's hole is great, boss," I said, and to my surprise, most of the lads laughed. Harry was po-faced.

"You wanna watch your tongue, son," he said.

I had taken the fight to Harry and, in my mind at least, won. *Sam 1–Harry 0.*

"You want me to stick to the left, then?" asked Toby, getting back to business.

"That is what I have been trying to tell you. None of this floating nonsense . . . if you want a starting place in the team."

Toby beamed.

"You're in, son."

"Yeah? Nice one, Harry," continued the shocked Toby. Mikey and I exchanged short looks of surprise, but not disapproval. Toby was good, and we needed him. Harry had made a bold decision, including someone he thought was "gentle" and lacked "sharp teeth" in arguably the most important game for years.

"Pretty Boy's hamstring is mashed," explained Harry. "You've just got your lucky break." Harry felt good about making Toby feel good.

And then I nearly fainted.

I was looking at Toby opposite me, genuinely happy for him, when I noticed someone walking into the park. He approached the football gang, but kept a good distance. Young, with a confident walk, wearing a hooded top and drainpipe jeans, he stopped and watched.

It was Him.

My heart went bananas, and I felt a little out of breath. It was definitely Him. What the hell was he doing in Surbiton, and what the HELL was he doing watching us in the park? I could just about see a smile on his face. He turned, slowly, and walked back the way he came. The color must have drained out of my face, because Toby looked at me with a very big and unusual frown. I squatted; I think I'd have collapsed if I hadn't. It felt very exciting, but also very scary. Him had come into another part of my life, he was no longer just the guy at the football, or a chance encounter at one of the country's busiest train stations, no — he was now part of my everyday. He might have been seen by people I know. He freaked me out. The lads were still talking shop, and I felt as though all the blood platelets in my body had decided to race each other to my brain.

Mikey's ludicrously passionate arguing was quite an enjoyable distraction. Mikey hated the fact we had to use cones for goalposts, and it had become customary for him to claim goals that were probably high and wide.

"We gonna get the goals up for some practice before the match?" he asked.

"The council are being arseholes. We only get the pitch and

changing rooms for official games, as per bloody usual," said Harry, who had just about got his breath back.

Mikey wasn't happy about a decision Morph made during the mini-match we had just played. "Because I'd like to say here and now, that shot was most definitely a goal."

Toby, who had darted back to make a goal-line headed clearance, was having none of this.

"Shut up," he said, smiling at Mikey's stubbornness. Here began a nasty row.

"It was a goal."

"It was at least a meter over."

"I scored."

"No, you didn't."

"I'm not arguing, it was a goal."

"It so wasn't, stop kidding yourself."

At this point, Mikey lost it. He shouted with the volume of a loudspeaker turned to ten, and the ferocity of a lion —

"LOOK, IT'S ONLY A GAME!"

The veins in his neck nearly popped, and his face went purple, spit hanging off his lips. Toby nearly laughed. Morph broke the silence, appalled at Mikey's sentiment.

"Tragic . . ."

"That attitude saddens me to the core," said Harry, glad to see Mikey put down for once.

"They take it so seriously," said Mikey. He was playing into Harry's hands now.

"Bloody right they do," started Harry, and I sensed this heralded his big motivational team talk in the final formal training session before the big game. "You wanna know why?"

"No," said Mikey. Harry didn't even look at him, and continued.

"'Coz they have hunger, they have teeth. Precisely what you're lacking, son. Get yourself some dentures. And stop all the squabbling. I need group harmony. Don't forget the alcohol ban I have imposed. As of today, anyone found to breach this will be subjected to a considerable fine. Now, Morph and me want you to begin to psychologically prepare for the magnitude of this Summer Cup game."

The regulars amongst us had heard this speech several times before. It was boring, although Toby seemed engrossed. I heard what Harry said, but didn't listen. I was temporarily unconcerned about the fact my teammates had been feeling uncomfortable around me. I was no longer all that bothered about Harry. These concerns went to the back of my mind. I was far more interested in thinking about Him. Imagining Him.

Mikey was picking his nose and flicking the contents onto the grass below. He couldn't give two hoots about Harry's textbook attempts to get us pumped either.

"Think of Glasgow Rangers against Celtic," began Harry, in a comparison that was ludicrously out of touch with the reality of our situation. That game attracts around sixty thousand spectators and features some of the strongest religious rivalry between two sides anywhere in the world. Our game would do well to attract a crowd of two hundred, and nobody outside of our town gave a shit. Still, we shared the same name as one of those teams, even if Glasgow is ever so slightly bigger than Surbiton.

". . . or think of Man U Man City, Liverpool Everton. It's the big one. As you may know, I used to play for Lockham until the . . . artistic differences." Mikey smirked at me, and even Trevor was trying to hide his grin from the management. Harry was clearly kicked out of Lockham for being an unreasonable arsehole.

"Well, my loyalties are firmly on our side of the fence now. We'll fight them on the pitches, boys, and we'll win. Teeth, boys, teeth!" finished Harry, attempting to emulate Winston Churchill but sounding more like a cable TV football commentator.

"Teeth!" screamed Morph, terminating the training session.

Toby had to go to the factory for an afternoon/early evening shift, so he left quickly, leaving me to hit the park toilet for a good half hour, feeling utterly overwhelmed, as had become the tradition. Although I had opened a door to Brenda and she was a bigger part of my personal life, the problems I was facing could only be resolved by me, and although her support meant everything, *I* was the one who had to do something.

The night before, and now the appearance of Him, preyed on my mind. I had plenty of questions, lots of confusions, few answers, fewer conclusions. I went to the Abbey for a couple of post-training drinks, which may have been in direct contradiction to Harry's alcohol ban, but, frankly, I needed and deserved some vice.

CHAPTER 17

SO IT COULD BE LOVE

After the shooters I came home, still not properly recovered from the previous night's drinking, to find a message my mum had left for me in the kitchen. Scrawled on a piece of paper was *Call Lucy, 7648226.*

What for? Why? Weird.

I took the portable up to my bedroom, chucked my kit bag on the floor, lay on my bed, and phoned. She didn't talk long, but said she was passing and would I mind if she dropped in. I was a bit miffed, but I told her she was welcome. Mum was at work, so I was home alone, listening to "True Faith" on my *Best of New Order* CD. I welcomed her in and we sat in the living room.

Lucy was looking very summery; a slight blue dress, sandals, and little else. She'd been in the sun (before Harry jinxed it), and a golden brown tan was seeping through the freckles dotted about her nose. She looked hot, and I sensed something horny about her when she arrived. It's in the eyes. Sometimes you look at someone's eyes and you have this strange — but exciting — vibe. Her pupils were playing games with my pupils.

It turns out she'd come over to see how I was. She said she felt really bad about how things had gone at Bliss. I told her not to worry, that it wasn't her fault, but she was adamant she'd make sure I was OK. Bless her.

Then we got chatting about all sorts of shit. Somehow we went from New Order to cartoon shows to the aquarium fish to the *Carry On* films, all in about five minutes. I love those sorts of conversations. As she started to talk about her favorite, *Carry On Up the Kybher*, I began getting all lost in her. I remember thinking, *I fancy this girl* — and not just to get back at Toby. Proper fancying. She had these big, dizzy eyes. Perfectly shaped, manageable breasts fitting snugly into her blue dress. Long and sleek legs that sparkled when the sun caught them. And smooth arms that led to a lovely neck. I remember having a split second of a dirty thought about what it would be like to kiss that neck, before feeling instantly guilty and returning my attention to what she was saying. I felt inwardly grateful that I fancied females.

She was telling me her theory that the *Carry On* films had a deep feminist subtext.

"My friends take the piss," she mused, "but the *Carry On* films are all fiercely feminist. Women always come out on top, and the men are made to look like idiots. It was well ahead of its time."

I was sort of half listening to her, half mulling things over in my head. I must have sounded like I was ignoring her, when quite suddenly I asked:

"Do you love Toby?"

She seemed a bit surprised, but she kept her cool.

"I don't know. I really don't. It's too soon to say, I suppose. We have fun, though. Why?"

Always answer a question with a question. I think politicians say that. So I did.

"Do you really like him?"

"Yeah, course . . ."

"So it could be love. Or it could become love. I'm not shit-stirring, but he's been quite a player in his time and I wouldn't want you to —"

She sensed what I was getting at. Toby's never been a player. At least, he's never cheated on anybody. I *was* being a shit-stirrer, and a naughty one at that.

"Sam," she said. "Do *you* love Toby?"

I got up off my armchair and walked nervously around the coffee table.

"No! God! How can you ask that?"

"I just did. Easy. I don't mind — do you or don't you?"

"I can't believe you asked that so willy-nilly."

"An answer would be nice."

"I like Toby a lot. He's my closest friend. We're very close. But love . . . that's a whole different fish." That was fairly honest of me. Although back then, I had no proper idea of what love was, or whether love and physical relations had to be linked. But my statement left me feeling a bit more relaxed, a little more cocky. I sat next to her on the couch. She pulled the hem of her dress down so that it rested half an inch over her knees.

"Closest . . ." she pondered.

"What?"

"Interesting that you said *closest* and not *best*."

"Interesting?" I tried not to sound too confused, too naive, or too clever. Not easy.

"Very. You think too much, Sam. It's sweet." Her voice changed at this point. So did her look. She too seemed to be relaxing and leaning back on the couch. "Look . . . what Toby and I have got is a fairly informal relationship. I mean, no commitments yet . . ."

She moved a little closer to me.

"Best way if you ask me," I said, not really knowing what I was talking about. "Open relationships must work . . . I mean, there's no point resisting temptation."

"No," she said, dreamily, moving even closer.

I continued. "Especially not when it's right" — our fingers locked — "in your" — we moved to within an inch of each other — "face. . . ."

Then our lips met, and our tongues introduced themselves to each another.

The kiss was accompanied by some warm and clammy fumbling hands. I held her face and felt her thigh and stroked her hair. She gripped my waist, then ran a hand through my hair, and slipped the other under my shirt onto my back. After a good minute of action, the snogging finished. We were both red-cheeked as we sniggered anxiously and took our hands back.

"Wow," was all I could think of to say.

"Yeah . . . wow," she said.

"Erm . . . that wasn't meant to happen," I said, lightheartedly, making eye contact. I secretly felt an enormous sense of achievement.

She laughed, and stood up.

"Sorry —"

I interrupted her:

"No, it's . . . I mean, I'm sorry . . . don't know what happened there . . ."

Embarrassment dripped off both our faces. Lucy's mobile phone rang. It was Toby. She sat back on the couch as I sprang up immediately and paced nervously about the room. I only heard her say, "Hello . . . fine . . . sure, eight o'clock . . . OK." She told me she had to get going, picked up her handbag, and just then my home phone began ringing. We stood still and looked at each other. The phone rang on.

"Are you going to answer that?" she asked me.

I really didn't want to, but reached for the phone all the same. It was Toby.

All Lucy would have heard was "Hi . . . thanks . . . great, yes . . . eight o'clock, OK . . . bye then."

I'm not sure why I abandoned all reason and agreed to go to the cinema with Toby, particularly when I knew Lucy would be coming too. I think he was trying to patch things up between us after the aquarium and Bliss clashes. But that night was most definitely not the right time.

We didn't talk about the kiss again — Lucy left quickly, and I made sure I arrived at the cinema just before the film started, to avoid any awkwardness with the happy couple. The evening was uneasy, but at least the gung ho American action movie prevented long periods of dangerous conversation and pregnant pausing. I gave the couple a quick farewell on the steps of the multiplex, and decided against planting a good-bye kiss on Lucy's cheek. Toby looked at me curiously as I darted off, leaving no time whatsoever for chat.

My toilet beckoned, and I thrashed out the day's events in slow motion, with several mental action replays. This is when it began to truly hit home that I was stuck in a rut and going nowhere. Something positive needed to be done. I had to change direction, or else risk everything. I was in a huge hole, and the harder I tried to dig my way out of it, the bigger the hole was getting.

CHAPTER 18

SICK (NOT SICKO)

A whole week passed, during which I ignored Toby's calls. I was in a complete hurricane of emotions and confusions by now; I was still embarrassed about how I'd behaved at Bliss, and felt uneasy about fighting Toby and then begging his forgiveness. I felt dreadful about snogging Lucy. It was only brief, and we both laughed it off, and she got on with things and it's no big deal, but still . . .

And then, of course, there was Him, who I refused to talk to anyone about (in any case, they would have thought I was mad). My mind was a battlefield, and the warring factions had declared an all-out, ruthless attack on each other.

So I kept myself to myself. Pod and I were virtual strangers by this point, and Mikey was very busy with work. I attended football training, put in a good performance, acknowledged but hardly spoke to Toby, and continued to feel as though the eyes of the team were all on me. I phoned a couple of uni friends, just to keep in touch, and they were enjoying themselves in far-flung parts of Yorkshire. They asked me how I was. "Fine," I lied.

I considered finding my trousers and fishing out Greg's phone number from the pocket, but I thought I'd wait a day or two. Whenever I thought of Greg, though, I felt a little better.

Brenda invited herself round to watch a video, but we didn't talk much. I was giving *kindly fuck off* vibes. My mum hardly noticed me, spending most of her time preparing for the big Summer Barn Dance with her line-dancing troupe. For me, these were some much-needed lazy days.

Eventually, after a week of this sort of existence, and the Friday night before the big Saturday Cup game, I came to the conclusion that I was being a coward, and phoned to meet with Toby at the Abbey. After about an hour of sitting on my bed, staring blankly, fidgeting, and closing my eyes, I came to a decision. I kept on hearing Greg in my head: *Don't worry so much about yourself*. He was right. But in order to stop worrying, something positive had to be done. The hole I had dug myself was getting out of control, and I needed out. The Church and Abbey would be the location, my friends the audience.

I invited Brenda to the Abbey too, and she said she wanted to bring Pod along, having swallowed her pride and called him up to "sort things out." I agreed through gritted teeth. Arriving deliberately early, I headed straight for the toilets. At about seven o'clock the toilets are still in a decent state; three hours later, there would be more vomit, piss, and bog roll on the floor than in the bowls. I put the lid down, made myself comfortable, and began contemplating how, among other things, I was going to tell Toby that I'd kissed his girl. That would be the first step — rid myself of any feelings of guilt and come clean.

Instead, I found myself thinking about terms to describe my sexuality. After the Bliss night, I had decided that gay bars weren't my thing. Or at least, "traditional" gay bars weren't my thing. Sure, there are far worse places on the straight scene, but the camp pop, glitter, tight T-shirts . . . just not my idea of a good time. Greg, however, was a far healthier strand of "gay." Plus he was a fireman. At the same time, I was beginning to decide what "love" meant, and was confident you could love without wanting a shag. Then, suddenly, it came into my head. Not bisexual, and not monosexual (although it's a cool word).

Trisexual.

I'll try anything once.

I flushed the loo and returned to the bar, determined to apply to my life Greg's advice to chill. But still I felt unsure, and as much as I tried to imitate Toby's swagger, I still resembled a bungling Charlie Chaplin.

I found a table and sat myself down at it with a pint of Bishop's Finger. I whipped out a Biro and scrap of paper from my jacket pocket and began doodling, just as Toby arrived. By now, I was in definition overdrive.

"Have you ever thought of yourself as a graph?" I asked him, recalling the struggle of school maths lessons. He looked at me like I was mad. "A parabola, right?" I said, drawing the u-shaped graph, which I had never fully understood. But it looked good. "The curve is the bisexual bit . . . I think I've got it, Toby. I'm parabolasexual. Or how about sexuality as a Venn diagram?"

He smirked. "Don't get so worked up about it. What're you drinking?"

I was in no mood for heavy boozing. Something weird came over me that night. The Lucy snog, which happened so soon after the punch-up, tipped me over the edge. I was babbling on a bit like a madman, not really aware of myself, nor able to stop. My plan to take decisive action was falling apart.

"And then I think," I started, ignoring Toby completely, "what is it I'm fancying? I mean, there are some very boyish girls and some very girlish boys out there. Look at us . . . we're closer than most to understanding the whole thing. But I'm still . . . still missing something." Toby drew breath to try to speak, but I continued. He sat down, defeated. "Keep telling myself I'm lucky, luckier than most anyway. Lucky to be at college, have a house. But then I'm unlucky to have to keep secrets, live a lie. Then when I get real down about it, I think, imagine keeping secrets living in a tiny shoe box, a crummy flat, imagine that . . ."

Toby told me off for being patronizing.

"Sorry, you know I don't mean to be. But it's true, we could be much worse off. It's all fate, I keep telling myself. Things happen for a reason. I'm single and celibate for a reason." We both smiled. I looked him in the eye. "But at least . . . I mean . . . I'm lucky we're friends." This I meant, and I had intended to tell him.

He smiled reassuringly at me. This was beginning to feel really positive, like he and I were defining our relationship at last.

"There's nothing wrong with feeling like you've got things bad," he said. "You've heard about the difference between a black guy and a gay guy, right? Black guy doesn't have to tell his parents he's black. I'm not saying we have to tell our folks we're gay —"

"'Coz we're not —" I interrupted.

"Yeah, but we're weird. It's not usual."

"It's not unusual," I countered.

"No, but . . . I dunno. Pod wouldn't get so narked if we were just normal friends."

An uneasy silence interrupted. I found a confidence to address the issue that previously I had lacked. The issue was no longer just about me, it was about the two of us. And I felt different.

"Why do you think we've never gone further?" I asked, not quite believing I'd asked it, but relieved I had, and pleased that I was able to be blunt about the two of us. What Toby had said the night that we brawled was absolutely right — it was about time I spoke to someone about "my problem," which wasn't just my sexuality but which was also my and Toby's friendship.

"I don't know. Maybe it's like you say . . . fate."

I didn't believe him. He knew why we hadn't gone further. Because he wasn't interested in me in a sexual way.

"I'm really alone, Toby," I said, happy I could confide in him again.

"I know you are. But, you know, I'm here."

"Thanks. It means a lot to me. But even so, it's like I'm always struggling, always by myself —"

At this point, our most touching moment since we first admitted our "unstraightness" to each other was shattered by the raucous arrival of Brenda, Pod, Mikey, and, to my surprise, Lucy.

"Interrupting something?" asked Mikey.

I told him to shut up. "Oooh . . . handbag!" he replied. Ha fucking ha.

We all exchanged hellos, although Pod avoided eye contact.

Lucy and I smiled briefly at each other, both of us filled with embarrassment and shame. She and Toby kissed on the lips. I felt instantly empty, gutted that our tender time together had been so abruptly cut short. Pod was fascinated.

"No one told me about this!" he said, wide-eyed.

"Oh sorry, Pod," began Toby. "I *did* put an ad in the local paper."

Mikey and Pod started up a Church and Abbey chant, which given the time, was odd, but then I realized they'd remixed the ending so it went:

"One Church and Abbey, there's only one Church and Abbey, one Church and Aaaa-bbey, but there are lots in Wales. . . ."

During the mystifying chant, I began to feel really out of it. It's hard to describe; it was as if I was out of my body, looking down on this pathetic pub scene. Looking at Mikey and Pod and Brenda and wondering how much I'd moved on since the truly lonely, dark days of school. Looking at Toby and thinking whether he'd been a good thing for me, or whether he'd tormented me to the point that I wanted to call off our friendship. Looking at Lucy and wondering why I ever snogged her. And looking at myself and realizing something had to give. I had to know where I stood, and make sure everybody knew where that was too. The real me looked blankly into thin air, and I knew I was doing it. Not for attention or words of comfort from Brenda, but just because I felt totally absent. I was fed up with the laddish chants, fed up with the lads. Fed up with the Church and Abbey and all its ales, bitters, lagers, and cheap white wine, its boys and girls "up for a large one," its stained carpet and yellowing striped wallpaper, its jukebox spewing out pop. I wanted out.

"Birds of prey!" screamed Mikey. "Sam, we'll find some bees of prey for ya, mate."

"Give it a rest," said Pod, causing heads to turn.

"What's up with you?" asked Mikey.

"I'm just getting bored of it. If he wants to be batty, fine."

"Charming," said Brenda, thoroughly disappointed in him . . . again.

"He knows it's a laugh, don't you, hotel motel?" Mikey asked. Nobody laughed. Pod grinned.

"Sam is sick," said Sam, possessed by something otherworldly, because little that I said in the subsequent minute or so was particularly planned. It just kind of happened.

"You're not sick, mate," said Mikey, trying to be kind.

"Oh yes I am. I'm sick of lying, and being lied to. Sick of being who I'm not, of pleasing people by saying what they want me to say, feeling how they want me to feel."

I was welling up. My eyes watered slightly, my bottom lip quivered, my voice faltered. But I felt so strong.

"Chill, Sam —" I interrupted Toby before he could convince me to stop. Although I'd been thinking these thoughts for a long time, and had indeed planned to stop the rot, and even coined one or two of the turns of phrase, I never intended to say what I said. I stood up, banging the table with my fist as I did.

"Sick . . . of being scared and alone. I may be sick but I'm not a sicko. What's sicko is living your life in fear of rejection, scared of your own mum, your own best friends. It's being made to feel unnatural, like a piece of shit because I'm not like you. Why should I feel guilty for your problems? I'm happy with what I am now, are you?" I looked at their faces — mainly shock, all of them stern. I had so much to say, I left them no time to answer. "Have you any idea how lonely it can be when you just can't be honest? When there's no one to talk to?"

My nose was running. I took a big sniff and looked at Pod. "When you were asking Brenda out, taking her to the school dance, and all along I . . . I wanted Josh and I just couldn't say. Well, now I can. These are the facts. I'm attracted to boys and girls. And that doesn't make me a slag or irresponsible, hedging my bets, confused, in denial, greedy. I'm just Sam. I was born like this. But I've not always been able to admit it. Well, I won't have it anymore. So if you wanna take the piss, stand up and be counted."

Silence.

"OK. So let me be myself without feeling so bloody scared. I won't be scared anymore. I won't put myself down, let myself feel worthless. I'm not worthless. I'm me and I'm proud of myself." I paused in realization. "For the first time I'm proud of myself, not what I've achieved in exams or football teams . . . proud of what I am. I've done it. Said my bit. I've lost years of love because I was scared. I've never had a relationship because I've never said my bit. Well, now I've said it, and I'm ready. Ready to love and be loved. And I won't be scared anymore."

No more tears.

Brenda's eyes welled up. She walked around the table and gave me a big hug.

"I'm so proud of you," she said.

"Piss off — you'll make me cry," I replied. We both sniggered.

Mikey stood too.

"This is OK," he said. "I can deal with this. I don't mind.

210

Really I don't. And I want you to know that. I'm sorry for taking the piss. I didn't think you actually were, y'know . . . upset."

This was all getting a bit much. Mikey getting emotional? "It's all right, Mikey," I told him. I noticed in the corner of my eye Brenda and Pod talking quietly but animatedly.

"Leave off, it's my turn," said Toby, and he gave me a hug. The events had overtaken me, and I was far too excited and nervous to feel any tension in this close moment with Toby.

"Well done, Sam."

"Your turn next," I said.

"I've not told any of my schoolmates. Good speech, though. Mind if I use it?"

"For a price, sure."

"Cheeky git! I mean it, though. Well done. What song shall I play on the jukebox?"

I told him to avoid anything by a boyband. As he walked to the other side of the pub, Lucy approached me. We spoke in hushed tones.

"Lucy, I wanted to — I'm sorry about the other night. We got carried away, I guess. . . ."

"Don't be sorry, it's not your fault," she said, smiling.

"Does he . . . suspect anything?" I asked.

"No, I don't think so. It was just a snog. It's not like it was anything serious," she said, trying to convince herself as much as anything.

"No, course not," I said, trying to convince myself as much as anything.

"But he has told me you've been a bit stressed. Judging by that, I think we can all tell why."

"Yeah, was a bit melodramatic, wasn't it?"

"It was brave. You've done a really important thing."

I felt a bit emotional again. Damn.

"Thanks, Lucy. As I'm on the honesty trip, I might as well say, I think you make a good couple. I mean, he's a good egg. You're a lucky girl," I said. And I sort of meant it. I felt a shift in my attitude towards her and Toby's relationship.

"Aww, thanks," she said, giving me yet another big hug.

I made the mistake of staring directly at Pod as I said, "I'm not doing badly here! Anyone else for a hug?"

He looked away as quickly as possible. I walked over to him, put a hand on his shoulder (briefly), and summoned up some more of that courage reserve.

"What's up, Pod?"

He looked dead ahead, flanked by Brenda and Mikey.

"Nothing's up," he said, fooling nobody.

"Are you all right?" I asked. He took a deep breath.

"I need a minute."

"OK. OK, I understand."

"I'll get a round in." Pod deflected attention, doing what he does best. "Usual?"

"Yeah. Actually no," I said. "No, I'll have a red wine. . . ."

Toby had put The Jam's "A Town Called Malice" on the jukebox, a suitably rousing and uproarious number for us to all sing along to. All, that is, but Pod, who seemed to be taking an age at the bar. I, on the other hand, was having a really good, sober time. I felt so — for want of a better word — *alive*. For the first time since I was a child, really alive and good about being alive. In fact, it felt a bit like being a child again. For better or worse, at least these friends knew me now.

About halfway into The Jam, Brenda disappeared. She found Pod at the bar and took him to a table on the other side of the Church and Abbey for a heart-to-heart. She was so worried about him — I knew she still cared for him, despite recent events. She knew Pod better than any of us. And thanks to my little crisis and revelation, she now knew him inside and out.

"So?" she told me she asked him. He was fixing his stare on his pint glass, avoiding her.

"I don't understand," he confessed. "My oldest mate. It just doesn't seem right, and I know that's out of order." There was a lengthy, painful pause. "It's not my fault," he said, and that must have taken some courage.

"I know. Just like it's not Sam's that he's into boys and girls, and it's not Mikey's that he wears white jeans."

Pod chuckled, which marked progress. "Things went a bit tits-up for you and me lately. I'm sorry," he said.

"You don't have to be."

"It's gonna take a while to get used to it. I can't promise anything, but I will try. I will try."

Brenda looked at him. He looked back.

"I love you," she whispered.

"Cheers."

Incorrect answer. She punched him lightly.

"Love you back," he said. "Not gonna run away, then?"

"Not now, no."

"Time for another?"

CHAPTER 19

"EVERYBODY'S GOT THEIR DUES TO PAY
I'M LOOKING SIDEWAYS LIKE MY MAN PELÉ"
— MCA, BEASTIE BOYS

I had avoided drinking more than a couple the night before the big game. But I was on such a high when I got home last night, I couldn't get to sleep until gone two A.M.

So here I am. It's now approaching twenty past six. The Big Match has been played. I'm on the toilet for, I've decided, the very last time. From now on, the cubicle will only be a place to take care of nature's calls. It's time to move on.

The day went so quickly — it was as action-packed as the summer that preceded it. Toby phoned in the morning and left an answer-phone message:

"Yeah, it's me. I got some big news for you, Sam. See you at the game, I guess."

I knew what it was. I could tell. I was first in the changing room (at last — somewhere to change). He arrived soon after. Just the two of us. In the changing room.

"I've dumped Lucy."

"Oh my God, are you all right?" I asked, probably sounding completely fake.

"It was little things she did that made me realize she could be so . . . immature. But she's younger, she's allowed to be. And she's going to Liverpool anyway. If it's not working, no use being a twat about it, let it go."

I was a little shocked at Toby's frankness. "But I thought you were happy?"

"So did I. But I was wrong. It's no big deal, we're still friends. I mean, a relationship that lasted a few weeks is hardly going to screw me up in the head. We were just honest with each other. I'm fine about it, don't worry."

I paused, looked at my feet, and breathed in. The final thing to get off my chest.

"I'd like to be honest now too. I should have said this ages ago. Well, not ages exactly, but . . . you see, the thing is, I pulled Lucy."

The reaction surprised me: His face turned into a picture of rage, he clenched his right fist, and came towards me.

"You bastard," he said, with menacing quiet.

"Sorry," I squeaked.

"Yeah, you will be."

He came up to my face then pretended to box me, without making any contact, just laughing.

"I knew that all along, mong-face," he said. I was relieved but, as ever, lost.

"What?"

"Well, for a start, it was obvious the way you acted all embarrassed around me when we went to the cinema. I knew something was up. And for seconds, Lucy told me."

"She did WHAT?"

"It's all right — she wasn't my property, we were hardly going steady. Besides, she always thought you were quite cute."

"Did she?" I asked, genuinely flattered.

"Oh yeah. But listen, you're welcome to her," he said, again being far too reasonable. "I mean, I don't mind if you wanna chase things with Lucy now."

"It was just a snog, I don't fancy her!"

We both laughed — it wasn't "just" a snog. But Toby's invitation was disarming and I felt different. Then a pregnant pause — the last pregnant pause of the summer. Toby went to softly punch my chin, but I grabbed his wrist and held it. I looked into those brown eyes for what felt like forever, but was probably more like five seconds. We were both neutral. Suddenly —

"Well!" blared Harry, scaring the bollocks out of us. He marched in, followed by Morph (wearing big, black aviator shades) and Mikey.

"What's all this, then?" asked Morph.

"This is the big match, boys. How can you concentrate if you're . . . being gentle?"

Toby was genuinely embarrassed. He'd never been caught red-handed before, and yet he wasn't doing anything that deserved any feelings of embarrassment.

"If you must, don't do it here, lads," said Harry, the smug bastard. Mikey suddenly turned a peculiar beetroot color.

"Sorry, it's not what it looks like," I said.

Morph wasn't interested:

"Looked pretty clear to us."

"Sorry," I repeated.

216

"Don't apologize to him," spat Mikey. At this point, the rest of the team walked in, possibly to the worst pre-match atmosphere they had ever encountered.

Their presence made me very hot-flushed. I fantasized that I would be dropped and probably subjected to a round of insults from every Ranger.

"What?" asked Harry, without looking at Mikey.

"You heard," said Mikey.

"I repeat: What?"

"Why should they be sorry? Jesus, you two walk round like you own the town, never mind the football team. They're all right and they don't have to do it in private."

"Says who?" asked a furious Harry.

"Says me. And I'm their mate. And if you don't like it, you can fuck off."

For the first time ever, I felt so proud of Mikey.

"It's OK, Mikey," said Toby, attempting to diffuse.

"I'm entitled to express my view, son," said Harry, almost accepting defeat.

"Well, if you must, don't do it here, son," said Mikey. Brilliant.

"Yeah, Harry, who gives a shit?" said Nathan, and I melted. That sense of approval meant the world to me. I was no longer hot-flushed. I was now totally overwhelmed with the realization that my teammates, and Mr. White Jeans in particular, were being so supportive. I never would have guessed.

"Don't wind me up before the match," Harry barked at Mikey. White Jeans definitely beat him for volume, though.

"You've wound *them* up enough — don't like the taste of your own medicine?"

Morph bolted up to Mikey. "You watch your tongue!" he squeaked.

"Piss off, Morph!" Mikey shouted, lunging a fist in the weasel's direction. A terrified Morph backed away. The lads quietly laughed as Morph looked fruitlessly at the coach for support. But then . . .

"And another thing . . ." Mikey bellowed at Harry. "I hate your bloody coat!"

Me and Toby kept a straight face, but the other lads cracked up. The taboo had been broken. Somebody had slagged off Harry's coat. It was, after all, fucking awful. Harry looked at his watch.

"Twenty minutes to kickoff. I'll deal with you later," he snarled at Mikey, who got on with changing.

Everybody chose a clothes peg and began preparing. Harry consulted briefly with Morph in whispers. I looked at Toby quickly; I think he was as pleased with Mikey's defense as I was, but I did wonder if White Jeans would ever get a place in the starting eleven again.

I was really chuffed with Nathan too, for standing up to Harry. I had put my team shirt on, and just taken off my jeans, when Laid Back approached. Standing there in my boxers, I feared the worst. Then I noticed he was in his boxers too.

"Sam, mate. I couldn't give a flying toss what you do in your bedroom. But would you please score a fucking goal today?"

I smiled, and Laid Back returned to his peg. Toby grinned at me.

I caught Chopper's narrow eyes, and looked away, uncertain.

"Yeah, go on, Sam," said Chopper.

That was all he had to say for me to know for sure that I properly belonged now. They had always liked me, always respected my abilities, and they were always my mates. But now they knew me, and didn't seem to give a damn. My fears that they would object to getting changed in the same room, that they would avoid hugging me to celebrate goals, that they would refuse to even talk to me, these fears proved unfounded. I'm not saying the boys aren't prejudiced, and I have no idea what they really think, but acceptance — on whatever level — is the important thing for me — and for Toby — at this time. And moments before the biggest game of the season, we were accepted. The years of anguish, the decision never to confront my feelings, and to avoid ever sharing them with the boys, suddenly felt completely stupid. I remember thinking of Pretty Boy Pete, and wondering what all the fuss was about. I felt as light as a bumblebee. Even if Harry and Morph were struggling, most of the Rangers had come good. OK, so Trevor and some of the others hadn't said anything, but for some reason I knew they were all right about it. I wanted to hug every one of them, but that might have been pushing the boat out a little too far.

Harry interrupted my blissful trance.

"Right, gather round, everyone, listen up. Here we are, lads. The big match."

He began pacing around the square changing room, looking at all of us in the eye, clutching the lapels of his sheepskin monstrosity as he delivered his final attempt at inspiration. I've got to give him credit — he's capable of putting setbacks behind him and getting on with the task in hand. Many people would have fallen apart after having their prize asset ridiculed in front of a crowd.

"The old rivals. The Summer Cup to play for. A good few

hundred expected in the crowd, and a score to settle. They've won three out of the last five. Time to redress the balance. I want commitment, I want strength, vigor, style, passion, teeth! This is big-boy football. And I want big boys."

Toby cracked up. Laid Back, me, and White Jeans followed. Harry stared coldly. We stopped laughing.

"This is your chance to prove something. Fight for it, and fight for yourselves. Don't just fight for yourselves, fight for the club. Fight, boys. Fight and win. Lockham are SCUM. What are they?"

"SCUM!" we all repeated, military style.

"Revenge will be sweet. What do we wanna do?" asked Harry.

"WIN!" we shouted back.

"How much do we wanna win?"

There was general confusion. Mikey shouted, "Loads"; I shouted, "A lot"; someone else said, "Yeah"; and I even heard a "Win!" which made no sense whatsoever. Not the most coherent pep talk.

"Never mind that," said Harry. "On your toes." He clapped several times, and we all hurried up in getting ready.

"Win, win, win!" reiterated the manager.

Mikey initiated the traditional annual chant of "We are the Lockham haters," which we all joined in with (although Toby was a little lost). We were psyched, amped, and ready to roll.

As we finished off our preparations, Morph shared with the team the doctor's advice that he wear the aviator shades to prevent him from scratching his eyes. "Hay fever season, you see . . ." Nothing about Morph surprised us by now. There wasn't even a grin, just universal acceptance.

The lads began to leave for the pitch. I could hear a little rip-ple of applause and cheering as they made their way onto the hallowed turf. Our support was arriving. Harry, meanwhile, decided it was time for a chat. He called me over, just as Toby was leaving. I wasn't up for further confrontation.

"I know we've not exactly seen eye to eye on things, son," he began.

"Oh, don't worry, Harry —" I said, edging away, before his interruption brought me back.

"No, no, it's only right I take my share of the blame for that. It's probably sixty–forty in your favor, but I'll take that forty per-cent like a man. The point is, I want you to know that we value you, Sam. We appreciate your football. Good luck, son. Bag a hat trick."

I could forgive Harry. He was, at least, attempting to recon-cile, even if he did it in his own peculiar way.

"Thanks, Harry," I said. And I meant it.

"Now let's get out there and WIN!" he screamed.

Morph grabbed my shoulder and, his aviators just an inch from my face, shouted, "Teeth, Sam, teeth!"

I left for the pitch.

The crowd must have been about two hundred strong. It was awesome, but then this has been a regular local event for decades. Not quite the mix of Camden Town or Soho, but there were plenty of families, teenagers, students, young kids, pen-sioners, and, of course, our friends. Even my mum was there, rather embarrassingly in her line-dancing gear. The Lockham support gathered behind one goal and on one side of the pitch, while the Rangers' fans occupied the grass behind the opposite

221

goal, and opposite side. There were even one or two banners — *Go Rangers* and *We Love Lockham*. Team groupie Melinda, wearing an impossibly short skirt and knee-high boots, waved a placard stating that *Rangers have better legs*. I noticed and waved at Brenda and Pod, who stood right next to Harry, Morph, and last-minute substitute Dario. Dario was fifteen, skinny, pale, and generally sick-looking, like something out of Dickens. This mini-Morph certainly wasn't an ideal substitute.

The ultra-nervous grown-up Morph frantically called me over to the bench because I had forgotten my shin pads. And as I turned to head back onto the pitch I stopped dead.

Standing before me, dressed in his geezer gear, was Him.

He was by himself, as far as I could tell. He had a navy blue baseball cap on, and his eyes seemed brighter and more dazzling than ever. He looked great.

I couldn't move or speak, and breathing regularly was still proving a tricky challenge. No one seemed to notice my temporary paralysis, and the ref wasn't ready yet, so I had a few moments. Moments with which to stand perfectly still, barely breathe, and look like a complete dufus.

"Hello," Him said.

My mouth was so dry. I managed to "hi" him back.

"Good luck," he said.

He spoke with a South London, nearly Cockney accent — exactly what I'd imagined. It suited him. For some reason, I suddenly wondered if he also liked T-Rex, pizza, beer, and bitter, as fantasized. He kept looking, as did I. He broke into a smile, as did I.

"Go on, then," he said.

And on went I, feeling a sudden surge of confidence and

222

excitement. I still didn't know who the hell he was, or why the hell he was there, or where the hell he lived, but I got the feeling it wouldn't be too long before I found all of that out.

I was absolutely buzzing and desperate to get on with the game — probably to get rid of all the chaos pottering around inside my head. Trevor, appointed captain simply because he was the oldest, won the toss and elected to kick off facing our supporters, in order to give us a positive start. The atmosphere in those minutes before kickoff was unbearable. I was confident, but the Summer Cup game always made me far more nervous than any other game — and Toby seemed uncomfortable too. We looked proud in our blue-and-white-striped strip, all shirts tucked into our blue shorts and our blue socks pulled up, shinpads neatly resting behind them. Not like Lockham, a shoddy bunch of piss artists and yobs in garish green kits. What we lacked in physical strength, we more than made up for in mental strength. At least, that's what I told myself as the ref, Church and Abbey landlord Freddie, blew his whistle.

We were off. The crowd trebled in volume, cheering and clapping. I became even more nervous, and couldn't help but keep spotting Him in the corner of my eye. It was as though he was watching me constantly, which he probably was. Thoughts zoomed through my head like cars on an open highway. For instance, I felt a little bit sad, imagining that Him was no longer that close-but-distant boy whose world I had created for myself. Would knowing him ruin that? And how on earth did he know I played for the Rangers? Just as I found myself losing anything resembling focus, Trevor found me with a speculative punt from the other side of the pitch. I laid it on for Laid Back in the center circle.

Sure enough, the first Lockham tackle came flying in on Steve King, who was sliced into the air. In total, we won twelve free kicks in the first half and gave away none. They were well up for winning, and well up for a ruck. I had a couple of good dribbles from the halfway line to the edge of their penalty box, before being hacked down by their midget center back, who found his lack of footballing talent no obstacle to winning tackles — he just pulled us to the floor with two hands. Harry instructed Toby to take the subsequent free kick, which he whacked straight into the goalkeeper's balls. There was much concern expressed for him in the noises the crowd made. The keeper went down, and midget cleared the ball behind for a corner. Toby received several pats on the back, but it was still 0–0.

While their keeper was tended to by Lockham's assistant coach-cum-physio, our boys noticed a verbal spat between Harry and the Lockham coach. Clearly they remembered each other from their playing days together, before Harry was ostracized and forced to join the Rangers. The Lockham coach is known only as "Coddo" — a reference to his godlike status in a former career as a cod fisherman. He is from Aberdeen, has a graying perm and goatee, and walks at a forward angle, as if he is permanently desperate to get somewhere.

"You wanna control your team," said Harry, defiantly.

Coddo, dressed in awful mid-80s shiny Gola tracksuit, took two steps and, his body posed at a forward slant, raised a pointing finger at Harry.

"Hey, pal . . . bollocks," he said, very slowly, in an Aberdeen drawl.

And with that, he returned to his bench and surveyed the game.

I was struggling to keep my mind on the match. Harry's interruption in the changing room and the appearance of Him had left me with a mad energy boost that, although helpful in a tiring football match, wasn't aided by the fact I was deeply, deeply worried. For a start, I began to wonder if I possessed some strange telepathic powers — Toby had broken up with Lucy, just as I had wished. Yet I felt no satisfaction, no joy, no smugness. Toby was single again, just as he was when I met him and when I got to know him so well. But I wasn't very excited. As the game continued — and my contribution became, sadly, more and more anonymous — I was, instead, beginning to form some really clear ideas. Suddenly, things seemed a whole lot more obvious to me, and the 400+ piece jigsaw was falling into place. And then, interrupting the daydream —

Laid Back swung a corner into the penalty box. Their tall center back nodded the ball out to the penalty spot, where I met it with a powerful volley. It screamed past their keeper and into the top right-hand corner of the goal.

I was Maradona. I was Pelé. I was Hercules.

Suddenly the off-pitch drama flew out of my ears, and in came the noise of the hundred or so wild Rangers fans. But above their collective roar, my mum's screaming sounded out. I looked at her and she jumped up and down, arms waving. It felt great. Him was clapping enthusiastically, but my view was blocked when the lads piled in for a celebratory hug. It was the best goal celebration I had ever experienced. As is the custom, they hugged me, but this time it felt so good, and so real. The acceptance they had displayed with such good humor in the dressing room was demonstrated on the pitch with equal warmth. Toby put his arms around me and held tight, quietly muttering, "Superstar" into my ear. And, big head aside, I did feel like one at that point. But it was all like an old bedroom in which the furniture has been moved and years of dust has gone airborne; I had all these emotions — most of them high — rushing about, waiting to settle. And I couldn't quite settle them, but they were definitely slowing down and looking to land.

As was the tradition, Morph was on hand to guard against complacency. . . .

"No complacency!" he bellowed from the touchline, as Harry excitedly stuck two fingers up at Coddo and accepted pats on the back from Dario, Pod, and Brenda.

About twenty-five minutes had been played by this point, and we were all confidence, raring to go and score another. And we did just that. Only minutes after the game kicked off again, a beautiful through-ball from Trevor at the edge of the penalty box was met by the deft touch of Chopper, who rarely shows up on the score sheet. But this time he obliged with a neat chip over the diving keeper. As is the case when Chopper scores (and he's only done so three times), we sang:

He's big, he's round, he bounces on the ground,
Chopper Chub, Chopper Chub.

Two–nil, and we were ecstatic. Harry hugged Morph, before realizing the implications of such a public show of affection and pushing him back. Brenda hugged Pod. I hugged Chopper. We were all united in our ecstasy, and also our collective loathing for Lockham scum. Coddo stepped up to the touch-line and addressed his goalkeeper.

"Hey, pal . . . bollocks."

Coddo's legendary bollockings were duly dished out, the result being a first half that contained several more highs and lows for us. It's actually painful to recall the blunders and howlers in detail. I think Harry put it best in the changing room at halftime, when we gathered for a slice of orange each and the application of several muscular-pain-relief gels and sprays. Laid Back, for the first time I could remember, didn't smoke a ciggy. I think even he was shocked at the halftime score.

Once we were all gathered, Harry kicked the door open, which would have had considerable dramatic effect had it not swung straight back into Morph, who was obediently following his manager. Some of the lads sniggered. Harry picked up the tray of remaining oranges and, in a rather clichéd act of man-agerial passion, threw it across the changing room, covering us all in bits of fruit. He was primed and ready for fury.

"Two–nil. Two nil you were leading. How could you throw that away? Never mind throw it away, go one goal down. Three bloody two, boys. Three BLOODY two! That's because you're silly, silly, silly." This was one of those rare occasions where every single Ranger was united in the knowledge that Harry was right. We had lost concentration and given away two sloppy goals in the space of ten minutes. That's inexcusable, whatever level you're playing at. Then an accidental handball by Chopper had given Lockham a penalty, which made it 3–2.

"Now look, I want you to ignore playing down the middle, and pass it to the wings. Mikey, it's up to you to swing those balls in. Don't you worry about Sam, he'll be there."

"Sam," Morph piped up, "you've got to be there." You could always rely on Morph to be totally unhelpful. Harry stood opposite Toby.

"Toby, I'm taking you off."

Poor Toby looked lost.

"We're bringing Dario on," said Morph. Dario, the youngster, looked as though he was being asked to head into no-man's land without a rifle.

"What did I do?" asked Toby.

"Don't take it personally, son. But if we're playing more crosses we need some crossers, not dribblers. Now, lads, you know the score, keep those balls high — they haven't got a lot of height in the back four. We can cause a bit of hokey-cokey if we keep 'em high. Stay positive, boys. Think victory, come on!"

Harry clapped. The lads shouted to psych themselves up. I looked at Toby, feeling very sorry for him. He must have felt like shit. We said nothing to each other.

The team gathered in a line behind Trevor, ready to win this Cup and regain some Ranger pride. But I was still not concentrating. The funny thing is, although I couldn't put together a proper thought pattern as regards the game, everything else was becoming brilliantly simple. Whilst waiting to leave the changing room for the second half, I remember thinking that, far from being delighted that Toby's relationship had ended, I was unmoved and numb. I wanted to feel excited, but couldn't. What had moved me far more that day was the appearance of Him at the touchline. As we ventured back onto the pitch, I saw Him once more, and he gave me a thumbs-up. I remember thinking that the way I felt at that exact moment was entirely different from the way I felt when Toby told me he was single again, which in turn was nothing like the way I felt when the lads congratulated me so heartily when I scored my goal. That dust was really taking its time to settle.

Within seconds of the kickoff there was another cynical Lockham challenge — this time on poor Dario. He was crunched by the Lockham left mid, a guy I recognized from the Abbey, famous for rowing with bar staff and spilling pints. Morph ran on with the medicine bag and applied some gel to Dario's sore thigh. Harry was furious with the ref.

"Ref! Ref! You gonna send them off, or do we have to book a bed at casualty first?"

"Sit down, Harry," replied Freddie.

"Send him off, then."

Trevor wasted our free kick from the Dario foul by blasting it towards the sun. Laid Back started laughing like a chimp while Trevor punished himself.

"Crap, Trevor! Load of shit!" he said. Lockham laughed at us. Suddenly, they had good reason to.

Having been so confident of a victory in the early stages of the game, we were now staring defeat in the face. And things quickly got much worse. Mikey was on a soaring run down the right flank, and, per Harry's orders, most of the team pushed up to support him. He was tackled with expert precision and Lockham played the ball forward with speed and ease. In a matter of seconds, there was a one-on-one between their butch striker and our butch defender. A thumping whack that Nathan could do nothing about made it 4–2 . With fifteen minutes left, we were crestfallen and lacking in any kind of morale or cohesion. Depression combined with jumble as I thought of Toby, and exactly what it was I should say to him at full-time. Harry, meanwhile, tried to rouse us.

"Focus, Rangers, focus!"

After the kickoff, Coddo was slipping orders to his captain on the touchline. It soon became apparent he was encouraging his young thugs to cheat by diving for free kicks left, right, and center. Fortunately, the ref saw through most of their deceitful attempts. Even Pod joined in with the cries of disbelief from Rangers supporters in the crowd:

"That was never a foul, get up, you raving hom!"

Everyone heard him. He looked at Toby and, appearing very embarrassed, mouthed, "Sorry, mate." Brenda went from seething to beaming.

We, on the other hand, were desperate. Nathan persisted in punting the ball up the field, expecting me to score a route-one, long-ball style goal.

Harry was not happy. "Silly silly silly! Selfish football. They wanna play over the top, they wanna play like they've got Alan bloody Shearer up front. Take it, go with the ball . . . NO!"

He was seriously peeved. I dreaded the changing room at full-time, when the teas and sandwiches were liable to be splattered across our heads. Far more dangerous than oranges. But as the game trudged along, I came to a firm conclusion, and one that I would have to share with Toby. Muddled together with the thoughts about him, and Him, were my desperate efforts to help the Rangers get a hold on the game. The harder I tried, the less fruitful the results. I began to hate myself for not focusing enough in the first half, for being self-indulgent when I should have kept my eye on the ball.

There were five minutes left. I was frustrated at a largely ineffective half — I'd lost a lot of balls, misplaced too many passes,
and any self-confidence the first goal might have given me had
gone. But I wasn't going to give up. I knew there was still the
potential and talent in our team to get a draw and force extra-
time. I knew my mum and Him were in the crowd and, frankly,
I wanted to show off. I found my second wind and yelled from
the halfway line for a goalkick from Nathan. His precise punt
came to me, and I controlled it, passing to Mikey, who did a
neat one-two around the gormless Lockham center mid. I
picked up the return and ran at their defense, disobeying Harry's
order to avoid dribbling through the middle, imitating an Alvaro
Cruz move I had practiced for hours. And I could hear the
Uruguayan muttering, "You are the hero, Samuel," like in my
dream, which freaked me out a little. I rounded three defenders
using all the skills I'd picked up as a kid — the shimmies, the
dummy passes, the turns — and found myself with only the
goalie to beat. He dived at my feet early, leaving me time to kick
it round his body with my right foot, and slot it into the empty
net with my left. The midget ran back to attempt a goal-line
clearance, but tripped over himself and landed in the net.

I had scored.

4–3.

Our supporters cheered louder than before, and this time I
could hear my mum yelp, "My son! That's my son!" Brenda
smiled at her; I blocked it out and felt nothing. There was no
time to think about anything other than bagging an equalizer. I
could see Him in the corner of my eye, but tried my best to
ignore Him, albeit temporarily.

With less than five minutes on the clock, I grabbed the ball from the back of the net and ran to put it on the center spot for a hasty kickoff. Lockham predictably took their time, and they passed it around one another slowly. Harry was pacing nervously, chewing his nails *and* fingers off.

"Come on, lads. To the death!" he belted.

"Teeth! Teeth!" said Morph.

And teeth we showed. I cleared my mind of nonfootballing matters, and all of us put in a superb team effort in those final minutes, winning several tackles and challenging their keeper on numerous occasions. I tried a powerful, long-distance effort, which the goalie palmed away. Even Trevor had a shot on target. Lockham were falling apart fast. But the clock wasn't on our side, and Freddie blew full-time, prompting an orgy of Lockham bodies in the center circle. They were delighted, and I guess they deserved to be, but I couldn't help thinking they hadn't won it — we had lost it. The cherry on top of their footballer cake came in the form of Coddo, who dived onto the writhing mass shouting, "Bollocks." What a knobbo.

We were devastated. I felt bad, but at the same time very high about recent events. We didn't receive a single handshake from this year's Lockham team, which I thought was bang out of order. So we made our slow way to the changing room, clapped and cheered by the supporters. Nathan had a tear in his eye, as did Laid Back — this is the effect football has on even the coolest guys. Brenda congratulated me (a very British thing to say, "Well done" to the losers) and said she and Pod wanted to meet up when I was changed. My mum stopped me and gave me a big hug.

"Well done, Sam. You were the best!"

"Thanks, Mum."

"And I want you to know something. I have no problem whatsoever with whoever it is you choose to love."

That dizzy feeling returned.

How did she know? Why was she saying these things? And why now?

"Pardon?"

"I found the flyer for Bliss in your pocket, and Greg's phone number. That's absolutely fine with me. You'll always be my son, you know, and that's all that matters."

"No, Mum, wait —"

"You don't have to explain yourself, darling . . . I understand everything. And I love you."

I couldn't believe this. Having been told nothing for nineteen years, my mother now puts two and two together and gets six. But I was relieved that she was cool with me fancying guys, and gave her a massive hug. The best hug of the summer.

"I've got to go, Mum. Debriefing."

"OK, darling, in you go. I just wanted you to know I'm very proud of you."

"Thanks, Mum," I said, and I'm not ashamed to say my eyes filled up a bit. She made her way out of the park.

I quickly scanned the dispersing crowd for Him, only to turn around and find Him standing right under my nose. That tingly current ran through my blood fast. He had really clean, clear skin, which wrinkled slightly as he smiled.

"Hard luck. Good effort, though," he said.

"Thanks. I'm Sam Smith," I said. Jesus. The second time I had done that. It was beginning to be a very embarrassing habit.

"I know you are," he said. "You going to the match next Saturday?" he asked, referring to Litton Park's first home game of the new season.

"Course. You?"

"Yeah," he said. "See you for a halftime hot dog, OK?"

I nodded. "Sure. A halftime hot dog," I repeated.

He smiled again, as he made his way out of the park, and I knew that seeing him again was going to be good.

The "Sam Smith" blunder aside, I surprised myself at how un-nervous I felt during the exchange. Quite suddenly, it didn't seem to matter so much if anyone saw me talking to him, or if my secret friend became a little less private. The dust was really settling on the floor now, and the old furniture was beginning to look brand-spanking-new again.

I went into the changing room, where my excellent mood was more out of place than an undertaker in a cricket team. Everybody was so down, it was awful. Harry and Morph stood at one end of the room, like a pair of doctors about to meet with a dead patient's family.

"You don't always have to score more goals than the opposition to win the game," began Harry. As his speech went on, he slowly made his way around the room, and Morph stuck close behind him, nodding in agreement.

"Boys, you've done yourselves proud. You've done me and Morph proud. You won the battle against yourselves, against your lack of ambition, of belief. Laid Back even gave up on his halftime ciggy. Seriously now, they might have won the silverware, but at the start of the summer you was nothing. A bunch of no-hopers with no dreams. Now look at you — strength,

234

flair, teeth. I've got big ideas for this team, boys. We can build on what we've got. We can build and win. Give yourselves a clap."

We did just that. Harry was as emotional as last year, when we lost 2–1 to Lockham in the ninetieth minute. But this year felt crueller; we were a far better side, and Lockham were a particularly nasty bunch of bad-mannered mongs. Next year would definitely be our year. Morph put a hand on his shoulder; Harry clasped it briefly. Sweet.

I grabbed Toby and we approached the gaffers.

"Harry . . . we just wanted to say thanks. We'd both be well up for playing during the season proper," I said, motioning at Toby, who I knew Harry was considering signing for the league campaign.

"Really?" said Harry, with never-before-seen puppy eyes.

"Really," confirmed Toby.

"I'm sorry for subbing you, Toby," began Harry, before Toby assured him it was OK.

"Bless ya, boys. It's been an eye-opener," said the boss.

"You're all right. Both of you. All right!" added Morph.

Filled with jubilation after such a horrible low, Toby went to hug Harry, but that overstepped the mark for the big man. He pretended to look at his watch and turned away. Mikey stepped in at the right moment.

"Come on, Harry, I'll buy you a pint." He spat it out, the row with Harry still fresh in his mind.

"I wouldn't say no. See you in the pub, boys."

As most of the boys followed Harry and Morph out, Brenda and Pod poked their heads round the door. It was just me,

Nathan, and Toby left. Pod went straight to the tray of post-match sandwiches and scoffed a few cheese and pickles.

"Well done, boys," said Brenda.

"Bad luck, Sam," said Pod, between mouthfuls. "You did well."

I was quite nervous of Pod, to be honest. Despite knowing him since he was a shambolic-haired boy, this summer I realized that I hadn't truly known him — or his Lockham High self — at all. So I was scared of the unpredictable, of what he might say or do now that the truth was out. *But sod it*, I thought. *If my mum knows and is cool about it, that's the important thing.*

Nathan packed his bag, shook my hand, said his good-byes, and made his way to the pub, leaving the four of us to it.

After Pod congratulated me, there was a brief silence. I could sense Brenda and Toby staring hard at Pod, who made proper eye contact with me for what seemed like the first time in an age. I put my hand out to shake his. He looked at my hand with a look of disgust. I was completely unsure what he was thinking, but he demonstrated aptly when he gave me a big hug. Yes, another hug. And it felt brilliant and I realized it was the first time we'd hugged each other.

"Cheers, Pod. Now go and get a round in," I said.

Brenda smiled.

"It's what I do best, mate," Pod told me. "Well done." Then, for the first time since the near-fight at the Abbey, he faced Toby, smiled at him, and said, "You too, mate. Good effort." And with that, he and Brenda, arm in arm, exited the changing room and made their way to the White Horse — a new location for us.

And so there we were. Toby and Sam, alone again. I took my

footy shirt off, standing there in shorts and socks, while Toby was already in his ordinary clothes.

"I'm sort of sorry," I said.

"Oh? What are you sort of sorry for?"

"Not scoring." He chortled at me. "I tried, Toby. I feel like I've let the side down."

"You did great. You scored two, didn't you? Come on, you were head and shoulders above the rest of the team."

"You reckon?"

"Course," he said, and I thought how great it was that, even if he didn't mean it, he cared about me enough to say it with such conviction. Sounds silly, but it meant lots to me.

"Well," I said.

"Well," he said. "Thanks for being there."

"Jesus, you sound like a musical!" And he did. But it was sweet.

"I mean it. We've got something different. And I like it. It's what I think I've always wanted. Girlfriends and boyfriends will come and go, but friends are forever — isn't that the saying?"

"Sounds cheesy enough, yeah," I said, making light of the situation, but only because I could. A few days previously I would have been too messed-up to muster up a smile. I was enjoying myself playing with Toby instead of the other way round for once.

"I mean it," he said, all seriously.

"Sorry . . . I mean it too. It's nice to be cared for, nice to care for someone." I was totally at ease now. I was convinced he felt the same.

"I'm going to be honest again, though. I thought I wanted more from you."

237

"I know," he said, as cocky as can be.

"You do?"

"Well, you hardly made a good job of covering it up."

"I s'pose not." I was slow and definite. "But the point is . . . I was wrong. More would have just complicated things. Earlier, when the lads walked in on us in here, I felt different. It wasn't tense like before, and during the match I made a decision. I don't want it to be tense. I don't want to be hung up anymore. I don't want to be confused about you anymore. And today I knew for certain. *This* feels really right. I can be what I want to be because I am what I am . . . and I've admitted it."

"So what are we calling ourselves? Not straight?" he asked.

"Who cares?" I replied. And I truly meant it.

"Love you," he said, softly.

"Me too. Love you, that is."

I leant forward and kissed him on the cheek, then hugged him. We held each other for a long time. No tears, no words, no regrets. Everything felt so clear, and the room seemed so much brighter than before. Everything felt brighter, and better, and less hostile, and I didn't want the feeling to end.

Eventually I decided to put a shirt on, and we both left the changing room. I told Toby I'd meet him in the White Horse, that I needed the toilet quickly. And here I am. In the cubicle down at the park. Today deserves a moment or two of reflection. I had confessed to Toby I'd snogged Lucy; been wrongly accused of "being gentle" with him by Harry; been accepted by Harry; scored two wicked goals; lost the Cup game; listened to my mum blathering on about a fictional boyfriend; spoken to Him and arranged to hook up for a hot dog; finally made up with Pod; and, at long last, sorted things out with Toby. I'm about to head into a new pub, the White Horse, which is Harry's local. He's invited the team for drinks on him. I'm looking forward to it, unafraid and ready to silence the piss-takers. I won't stop going to the Abbey—it's been my local for the past four years, after all. But sometimes it's worth giving a new place a chance. It's time to try something new.